All the Way Home I'll Be Warm

Yolande Kleinn

Published by Yolande Kleinn, 2024

www.yolandekleinn.com

All the Way Home I'll Be Warm

By Yolande Kleinn

Book Design: Yolande Kleinn
Cover Photo: Tim Bish // unsplash.com/@tjsocoz
Cover Font: Cosmic Furry from thehungryjpeg.com
Cover Font: Kano from thehungryjpeg.com
Interior Font: Born from thehungryjpeg.com

First Edition December 2024

Print ISBN 978-1-946316-54-7
Digital ISBN 978-1-946316-53-0

chapter one

By the time his engine finally gives up on life, Jamie Phipps can't pretend even to himself that he's surprised about it. He has no survival skills when it comes to cars, but even he knows a vehicle shouldn't be making the noise he's been ignoring for the better part of five hours. The bumpy, uneven squeaking has been getting louder all day, bringing all kinds of other cranky behavior along with it.

Even the power steering has been uncooperative, and okay. Look. Jamie knows that's dangerous. Just like he knows he should've pulled over and found a garage ages ago.

But he's only an hour out from his sister's place—and only three hours beyond that from the Twin Cities, hoping like hell to make it that far before having to face the inevitable. He's barely left Fargo behind him, and he's *so close*. After two days on the road, he's more than ready to be done.

If he'd made it all the way home, he would've had weeks to deal with whatever the hell has gone wrong with his car before making the return trip back to campus. Easy. Simple. Probably expensive, but at least he could handle it all from the comfort of his parents' living room.

Instead, Jamie is stuck on the side of the highway, maddeningly close to the nearest off-ramp and terrified the gusting flurries of snow will make him invisible to oncoming traffic, even with his hazard lights on.

At least he managed to make it to the shoulder before losing momentum. He's safely past the rumble strip at the edge of the road, his windows fogging over as he waits on the line for someone from roadside assistance to take his information. His parents maintain a premium plan, and even so he's been on hold for what feels like an eon. Bad weather combined with the fact that it's only four days until Christmas, probably fucking up a lot of people's travel plans.

All the Way Home I'll Be Warm

He's glad for the thick winter jacket that he squirmed back into while waiting. The sun has just finished setting, and icy cold has already begun to permeate his little car. Fuck knows how long he'll be stuck here, but at least he can bundle up enough to be confident he won't freeze.

When he finally gets a human on the line, the news is even worse than he anticipated. His name goes on the list—and they'll get to him in about six hours.

Fuck. He hates the thought of begging his sister to save him. It's not like she's got any time to spare, getting ready for the holiday with a three-year-old while she and her wife are working full time. He could call his parents, and they'd probably bundle right into the car and come to his rescue, but that's a four-hour drive at best, just to reach him, and they're busy too. Getting ready for not just the usual influx of family, but for an extra guest who will be staying for the foreseeable future.

Jamie's more than a little curious about his dad's best friend. He's been hearing stories about Victor Leone his whole life, a mysterious figure so busy and absent that he has no idea what the man looks like. Victor's imminent arrival has Warren Phipps so excited that Jamie can't bear the thought of interrupting his parents' preparations. He'll figure something else out, and update them once he knows what's going on.

Waiting six hours is not a plan though, so Jamie does some extra digging. He hasn't made it too far past Fargo, and the map on his phone proclaims he's right at the edge of a tiny, middle-of-nowhere town called Mayworth. The place has a garage and a population of a couple thousand people. Even better, when he calls the garage's number, they're still open.

"We'll send the truck out to tow you in," says a graveled alto on the other end of the line. "You okay to stay put there?"

"Yes," Jamie breathes, slumping in his seat as the worst of the anxious tension bleeds away. "Thank you. I'll be here." He hangs up with a sigh of relief, probably more dramatic than the circumstances warrant, and dials his mom's number to give Anika Phipps the unfortunate update.

*

All the Way Home I'll Be Warm

The mechanic who comes to collect Jamie gives him a pitying look when he admits he hasn't even bothered to pop the hood.

Jamie shrugs, sheepish but unapologetic. It's not like looking at the engine would've told him anything. He knows how to refill his windshield wiper fluid, and how to check the oil. Everything else is above his pay grade, and staring at a broken engine block would've been exactly as helpful as trying to build a space shuttle from scratch: so far beyond the realm of reasonable expectation as to be comical. No way in hell was Jamie going to stand outside in the increasingly heavy snowfall, just to claim he tried.

The ride into town—only about fifteen minutes back the way he came—is blessedly short. Jamie is so relieved at not being stranded on the side of the highway that he takes the news with genuine calm when, once back at the garage, the mechanic's jargon-filled explanation ends with, "We don't have the right parts. I can place an expedited order, but the holiday really screws up delivery times."

"How long?" Jamie asks, already considering logistics. If he can catch a bus as far as Fergus Falls, his sister can surely make space for him to tag along the rest of the way.

"We should have it done and ready for you by the thirtieth. Nothing we can do to get you back on the road sooner. Sorry, buddy."

Jamie signs paperwork and slips the fob off his key ring, handing everything over with a sense of quiet inevitability. "Is there a hotel nearby?"

"Sure is." The mechanic scrubs a hand through messy hair. "You can get there on foot. Downtown's just a few blocks east."

The directions are so straightforward that Jamie doesn't bother jotting them down—just shrugs into his messenger bag and pops the handle up from his obscenely large rolling suitcase. He spares only the most idle moment wishing he had packed lighter for this trip. That was never an actual option, considering he's going to be staying for the entire month of January, but rolling a heavy suitcase on tiny wheels over sidewalks covered in deep snow…

This isn't Jamie's idea of a good time.

All the Way Home I'll Be Warm

By the time he reaches the hotel, he's talked himself halfway into a panic with the thought that they won't have any rooms available. It's four days until Christmas, and this is the only hotel in town. It's a locally owned place, small and cozy, and Jamie's heart is hammering from both exertion and nerves as he steps across the lobby threshold—grateful for the blast of warm air—and lets the door swing shut behind him.

A reception desk stands opposite a single couch and a roaring fireplace, the ceiling above stretching high with visible wood beams. The tiny wheels of Jamie's suitcase squeak, leaving wet trails on the thin carpet, as he makes his way across the narrow space.

Before he can ding the silver call bell, a round and smiling woman appears from an open doorframe beside the desk. She's dark skinned and pretty, with a face that looks too young for the striking sweep of silver curls tucked back from her face.

"Welcome to Woodhouse Inn. Do you have a reservation?"

Jamie cringes, and stumbles awkwardly through an explanation of his journey, feeling with acute awareness that he is oversharing and yet somehow unable to stop the words from pouring out of his mouth. Because no, he doesn't have a reservation. But he also has nowhere else to go.

The receptionist—*Shana*, according to the tag at her lapel—types quickly into the computer on top of the desk. "We're full up tonight, but I might be able to swing something."

Jamie blinks, torn between hope and confusion. "I... That's great but... How?"

"The owners have family in town for the holiday. Lots of family. That's most of the guests right now. Someone might be willing to double up."

Incredulity widens Jamie's eyes and makes his chest feel tight. "Why would they do that?"

Shana gives him a sympathetic look that is, thankfully, not quite as pitying as the mechanic's. It's kind and piercing at the same time, and Jamie finds himself wondering with a sudden burst of self-consciousness what he must look like right now. He's been driving for the better part of two days, trying to cram a twenty-plus hour trip into as short a duration as possible. He stayed at a hotel last night, but didn't sleep nearly long enough before hitting the road this morning. His limbs ache from hours behind the wheel of his car, his lanky frame tense from the road. His shirt started the day crisp and sharp, but he's hopelessly rumpled now. Even his hair—a mop of loose brown curls that are difficult to style under the best circumstances—is a chaotic mess after the wet and windy walk through what passes for downtown in Mayworth, Minnesota.

"Do you have somewhere else you can stay tonight?" Shana asks, still wearing that painfully kind expression.

"I... no."

"Then let me see what I can do." She gives him a reassuring smile. "There's a bar next-door, if you need something to eat while I get everything sorted. What phone number can I use to reach you?"

chapter two

Jamie leaves his bags with Shana behind the reception desk, then steps out into the blustery night. It shouldn't be possible for the air to feel even colder, but he's shivering by the time he reaches the next building over. His coat is more than thick enough to keep his core warm, but his well-worn jeans offer little protection against the bitter wind.

The bar is a long, narrow pub, dimly lit and charmingly garish. Dangling light fixtures hang at intervals from a low ceiling, covered by stained-glass shades that cast scattered fragments of rainbow across tables and bar top and dark walls.

A sign near the door proclaims, *SEAT YOURSELF*, so he navigates past a handful of other patrons and claims a table near a swinging door that probably leads to the kitchen. A server approaches quickly, and Jamie orders a basket of fries and a glass of hard cider he plans on nursing as slowly as possible, since he has no idea how much time he'll need to kill. He's not so much worried about the money, but he'd just as soon stay sober tonight.

Between eating his fries and trying to be subtle about people watching, Jamie calls his sister. Claudia will be home from work by now—though when she answers, her distracted tone and the occasional admonishment to *Please leave the food on the table, little love,* tells him he's managed to call in the middle of dinner.

"I can call back," he offers. He doesn't want to be a pain in the ass, and fielding a phone call while trying to convince a three-year-old to eat without making a mess seems… Well, as multitasking goes, Jamie's not sure he'd be able to pull it off.

"Nah." Claudia sounds a little more present now, while in the background Jamie hears his sister-in-law mutter something about carrots. "Lou's got this. What's up?"

All the Way Home I'll Be Warm

"Just wondering what time you guys are leaving for the Cities tomorrow."

"Probably around two," Claudia says, as Lou's running commentary from the dinner table fades to more of a distance. "Why? You okay?"

"I'm fine," Jamie says. "My car, on the other hand…"

"What happened?" Claudia's voice sharpens, and Jamie realizes she's probably assembling a picture in her head that's far more grim than his situation actually warrants.

"The engine died. I made it to a garage, but they need to order parts."

"Do you want me to come get you?"

"No." Jamie realizes only belatedly that he should've checked bus schedules before calling her, but he still feels confident in proclaiming, "I'm pretty sure I can catch a bus and be on your doorstep in time to tag along. You don't need to go out of your way."

"You sure?" she pushes, and that overprotective older sibling tone has crept into her voice. "Where are you right now?"

"Checking into a hotel in Mayworth," he says in a burst of optimism. He's not confident she'll know where that is but then, this tiny piece of nowhere is only about an hour from Claudia's tiny piece of nowhere, so anything is possible.

"Jamie, that's so close. I can make the drive tonight, it's not a big deal."

Her sincerity is unmistakable, but Jamie's gut clenches at the thought of his sister— probably already exhausted from a long day at the clinic—navigating this increasingly nasty weather and holiday traffic to come collect him. Even before his vehicle died, he was seeing a steady increase of cars in the ditch. Stubbornness and the desire to be home were enough to keep him on the road, especially as he moved east toward what he hoped would be the outer edge of the storm. But he's not going to ask Claudia to drive straight into all this, in the dark, when he has other options.

"Don't worry about it," he insists. "Really. I'll call if the hotel falls through, or if the bus doesn't work out."

"Why would the hotel fall through?" she asks, and Jamie can practically hear the way her brow is creasing right at the center. Damn it. He didn't mean to admit how dubious his prospects actually are.

"Long story," he says. "I gotta go. Give Lou and May hugs for me."

"Hug them yourself," Claudia says fondly. "We'll see you tomorrow. Unless you change your mind and want to be picked up tonight. *Call me if you change your mind*, okay? I'll keep my phone on."

"Will do," he promises. "Love you."

"Love you too, kiddo."

He texts his parents instead of calling them, painfully aware that if he gives them any opening at all, they'll insist on coming for him, interminable drive or not. Eight hours total, between reaching him and returning to the Cities. Easier to shoot down the inevitable offer in a text message, and he does it with as much grace and gratitude as he can convey with a winking face and a variety of heart-shaped emojis.

He's still gotten no word from Shana next-door by the time he finishes the giant basket of fries, but a distraction steps into the bar before he can fall down a fresh worry spiral. Jamie stares—incapable of subtlety and praying his shadowy little corner makes him inconspicuous—at the gorgeous stranger who strolls into the restaurant and claims one of the empty stools at the bar.

The man's ash-and-silver hair is just long enough to look tousled when he drags the knit cap off his head and stuffs it into a pocket of his coat. He wears a soft half-smile, and his prominent jaw is scattered with stubble almost thick enough to be called a beard. When he tugs off a pair of dark leather gloves, the hands beneath look big and blunt and strong.

Jamie's surprised by how tempted he is, to walk right up to this total stranger and start a conversation. He's not usually one for introducing himself to people. Social anxiety is a force to be reckoned with, and he's far more likely to ease into friendship sideways, through mutual acquaintances and other pretexts.

He's even more shocked at the instant zing of interest rushing through him. He doesn't usually recognize an attraction until he knows someone well enough to stop being a bundle of nerves around them. The urge to do something about it leaves him a little unsteady.

But hell, if he makes a complete ass of himself, who will ever know? It's not like he'll spend any more time in Mayworth than necessary to get where he's going and eventually come back for his car.

Despite this lack of consequences, Jamie can't quite bring himself to approach. Yes, he feels braver than usual at the prospect of flirting with a stranger—but he's not exactly in top form after two days of driving—so he settles for studying the newcomer more discreetly, considering the possibility but ultimately keeping to himself.

The man is stocky, probably shorter than Jamie, but built broad and powerful. His wide shoulders look like they can support more weight than is strictly reasonable. A moment later, when the stranger shrugs out of his jacket and drapes it over the high back of the bar stool, Jamie's mouth waters at this even better view. Muscular arms stand out distinctly beneath a dark t-shirt. Jamie would be shivering his ass off if he tried to exist in this space with so few layers, but the pervasive chill doesn't seem to bother the man, and Jamie is glad. He appreciates the unimpeded view.

It's impossible to tell how old the stranger is. Older than Jamie, certainly. Maybe in his forties, maybe more. There's something rugged and completely at-ease in the loose posture, the chaotic hair, the mouth perpetually quirked into the hint of a smile. Jamie stares at the handsome face in profile, the thick neck, the silvery stubble—and blushes imagining what that stubble might feel like against his skin.

It's a pleasant fantasy, nebulous and idle though it is.

And then the man pulls out a book—a skinny paperback that materializes from a deep pocket of his coat—and Jamie's heart does a happy little skip. He doesn't have a book with him now, because he was too flustered to dig anything out of his luggage, but he's always been the member of his friend group most likely to squirrel himself away with a ratty old pulp sci-fi paperback. It isn't just the instant kinship Jamie feels for someone who reads books in bars that sparks an unexpected affinity, but the book itself. It's a Philip K. Dick collection—a favorite Jamie has always shared with his dad—and even the cover is the same soft, surreal abstract design as Jamie's edition.

Quick as that, Jamie's initial attraction makes way for a softer, more personal curiosity. He picks up his jacket and his half-full glass of cider, and crosses the room to claim an adjacent stool.

"That's one of my favorites," he says, letting cheerful enthusiasm light his face into a grin.

"The book or the stout?" the man answers, so quick and teasing that Jamie wonders if maybe his perusal didn't go unnoticed after all.

"The book." Jamie sets down his drink and his jacket, then extends an open hand. "I'm Jamie."

The man considers him for a moment with an amused expression, one eyebrow quirked just a little higher than the other, mouth twitching at the corner. It could be the first hint of a flirtatious look. It could be incredulity presaging gentle discouragement. Jamie can't tell, but he hopes like hell it's the former.

"Sam," the man says at last, and accepts his offered handshake. "And I've never read it before. A friend sent it to me for a birthday... too many years ago. I'm trying to read it before I visit him for Christmas."

Jamie snorts a laugh. "So you're basically cramming for the test."

"Guess you could look at it that way."

"I could give you some pointers," Jamie says. "I've read that book at least ten times."

Sam's smile transforms into something new—wide and real—and quick as that, Jamie feels like he's passed muster. Sam isn't just humoring him now. They've crossed some threshold of camaraderie. Even better, Jamie has a name to go with the gruff jaw and those kind eyes that have begun assessing him with unconcealed curiosity. Jamie can't tell if there's deeper interest in the flicker of Sam's expression, but that's okay. He's not entirely sure of his own intentions here.

"I'm traveling for Christmas too," Jamie says, barely resisting the urge to ask if Sam is from around here—grudgingly aware that it would be easy to overstep the bounds of casual flirtation with invasive questions. "I'd be on the home stretch if my car hadn't broken down. Now I gotta wait until tomorrow and catch a bus to Fergus Falls."

"Shit. Sorry about your car." Sam blinks and gets a considering look. "We must be staying at the same hotel."

Not local, then. Jamie lets himself lean a little closer into Sam's personal space—not quite enough to bump their shoulders together—but enough to savor the glow of shared body heat. The fact that Sam is from out of town only heightens the sense that they're ships passing in the night, and Jamie doesn't think he's imagining the way Sam inclines just slightly closer in return.

"Must be," Jamie agrees, hoping he hasn't delayed in answering long enough to make things weird. "There's only one. I'm waiting for them to call about my room." He does not mention that this is still more hope than certainty. The last thing he wants is to make Sam feel bad for him, especially when Jamie's busy fantasizing about climbing him like a tree.

Thank god Sam breezes past this observation without further comment. He asks about the book. And about the tragedy of Jamie's car. And about the faded-out video game logo on Jamie's sweatshirt.

It's startling how easy Sam is to talk to. Worse and better and infinitely more distracting, Jamie feels the crackle of attraction sparking hotter beneath his skin with every word and glance. He edges farther into Sam's space, oblivious to the passage of time, gratified at the way Sam leans in just as surely to meet him.

Their bodies are having a whole separate conversation from their words, suggestive and cautious and quietly eager. And Jamie would very much like to unite the two conversations, at the same time as he's trying not to be an absolute brat about it. Despite his best efforts to play this cool, he can't stop his gaze from dipping low, again and again. To Sam's mouth. His hands. His muscular forearms resting on top of the bar.

At least Jamie has caught Sam's eyes wandering too. There's no way he's imagining this.

There is something increasingly self-conscious in Sam's manner, the more brazen Jamie becomes. A guilty flicker whenever Sam catches himself staring at Jamie's mouth. A tension in wide shoulders that wasn't there when Jamie first sat down. A growing impression that this isn't Sam's usual scene— that he isn't accustomed to picking up guys in bars—is perhaps even less used to it than Jamie, for all that he doesn't shy away.

All the Way Home I'll Be Warm

Jamie refuses to be dissuaded by the fact that Sam might be literally twice his age. He's been with people significantly older than him, and in his experience *they* usually have more qualms about the disparity than he does. It's going to be on Jamie to bridge the narrow ravine between them. Whatever Sam's hesitation, if he's interested in more than conversation, he clearly means to wait and see what Jamie will do.

Even once he recognizes that the next move is on him, it takes Jamie time to work up his nerve and set a tentative hand to Sam's arm. The touch is both a testing of the waters and a shameless excuse to feel the sturdy muscle of Sam's biceps. And well. Fuck. For such a sweet teddy bear of a man, Sam's got the size and strength to be a completely different kind of bear.

Sam relaxes into the touch, and when he leans even closer, Jamie's heart races at the encouragement.

The question of whether he dares to kiss Sam—a question that feels almost rhetorical with how little space remains between them, and how earnestly they're studying each other—

is rudely interrupted by the discordant melody of Jamie's default ringtone. He bites back a curse as he retreats in order to answer.

"Hello?"

"This is Shana at Woodhouse Inn. Am I speaking to Jamie Phipps?" The pitched professionalism of her tone is completely different over the phone than in person, though it relaxes a little when Jamie confirms his identity. "We've got everything sorted over here. You can come check in whenever you're ready."

"I'll be right over," Jamie says, even though the thought of walking away from this bar makes his insides ache.

When he raises his eyes to Sam's, the intimate playfulness from a moment before has vanished in the face of clumsy reality. God damn it. If he asks for a kiss now, it will be painfully awkward. Maybe still welcome, but Jamie's confidence has evaporated with the wisps of the private moment they were sharing.

Instead of crowding back into Sam's space, Jamie swallows hard and says, "I should probably go." He offers a sheepish but honest smile as he sets a hand to Sam's wrist. "Thanks for the conversation. It was really nice to meet you."

All the Way Home I'll Be Warm

He startles when Sam's hand covers his own, holding it in place. The touch is gentle—Jamie could easily pull free—but there's something determined in the point of contact. Jamie meets Sam's eyes, and finds a flash of purpose there, so heated it takes his breath away.

"I enjoyed your company. If you..." Sam's voice sounds husky, even beyond the rumble of gravel that's been there this whole time, and the sandpaper roughness intensifies as he lets the sentence trail off unfinished.

Jamie furrows his brow, but his heart is suddenly racing. "If I what?"

Sam's posture straightens, like he's consciously bolstering his confidence to say, "If you need a distraction tonight, I'm in room twenty-three." As soon as the words are out of Sam's mouth, he looks ready to walk them back and apologize—like he's braced for Jamie to be offended.

"Really?" Jamie grins, shivering with delight "What time?"

"Anytime." Sam looks distinctly winded, but pleased by Jamie's answer. "I'll be turning in as soon as I settle my tab."

Settle my tab. As though Sam hasn't been ignoring his drink as thoroughly as Jamie's been ignoring the half-finished glass of cider, both too caught up in each other to bother with silly details like beverages.

But Jamie nods and tosses enough cash on the counter to cover his own bill with a generous tip. When he withdraws his hand, he detours just long enough to give Sam's powerful biceps another appreciative squeeze before he makes himself head for the door. *Room twenty-three* loops through his brain on repeat, stubborn as a song lyric as he navigates the burst of icy air between bar and hotel—as he gives Shana his credit card and thanks her profusely—as he hauls his bags up a single flight of stairs to the room that is miraculously his for the night.

He's already in a good mood, but he feels even better after a shower and a clean set of clothes. Not pajamas. Not when he still has places to be.

A significant portion of his mind can't believe he's going to do this. Never mind the inevitable safety concerns that come along for the ride whenever it comes to trusting a stranger—Jamie shuts those down easily after all the ways Sam spent their conversation being sweet and startled and unsure. It's just so far outside his usual patterns. He's about to sleep with a total stranger. Hopefully.

But there's something about Sam. Something beyond the shield of anonymity and the surety that Jamie will never see him again. And as Jamie pockets his room key and slips into the hall, his heart gives a pulse of excitement at what he is about to do.

chapter three

Jamie knocks on Sam's door with a fresh spike of anticipation, thrilling at the flutter in his stomach, the burn of impatient energy beneath his skin.

The door swings inward, and he grins at the pleased surprise on Sam's face. It should not be so goddamn charming, the way this man who *invited Jamie to his room* looks genuinely shocked that his invitation has been accepted. And yet Jamie can't help thinking it's sweet, that his acceptance wasn't taken for granted. That they've both been occupying this restless piece of common ground.

"I feel like I should offer you something to drink," Sam says as he closes the door with a quiet click, "but aside from the minibar, I don't really have anything. And I don't want to get you drunk if we're going to..." He tapers off, looking mortified with himself. Too much candor apparently, even though they understand each other well enough that Jamie is *here*.

Jamie huffs a soft laugh, startled at how easily Sam's clumsy candor burrows into his heart. "I don't want a drink," he says. And then, unwilling to let even the faint suggestion of awkwardness slow him down, he sets the deadbolt on the door. It's a deliberate gesture, if not especially suave—Jamie Phipps does not have a single suave bone in his entire lanky frame—and then he slips right into Sam's space, a shiver of hopeful expectation speeding his pulse.

He was right, in his estimation from the bar. Sam *is* shorter than him. And Sam's brown eyes are even more expressive up close, deep and interested and reflecting the lamplight from the corner of the room.

Jamie feels like he's impersonating someone confident and audacious when he admits, "I wanted to kiss you right there in that stupid bar."

All the Way Home I'll Be Warm

A delighted smile breaks across Sam's face. "I promise you, the feeling was painfully mutual."

And even though it's difficult to hold his tongue, Jamie does not let himself say the, *I don't usually do this kind of thing,* that wants to sneak out like a confession. He's here. He wants Sam to touch him. The last thing this moment needs is a protest Sam might mistake for reticence, when everything about standing here in a stranger's hotel room feels like the most perfect and inevitable decision Jamie has ever made.

He does not let himself overthink his next move. Nothing in his entire life has ever been as easy as reaching for Sam now. Jamie frames Sam's face between his hands, savoring the stubble-rough brush of beard against his palms. Such overwhelming intimacy in this moment— in the way Sam's sharp inhale is followed by a stillness that suggests Jamie isn't the only one holding his breath—and all of it twisting hot and sharp between them, despite the fact that they are barely touching.

Sam's mouth, when Jamie allows himself to lean in—an instant or an eternity later, he honestly can't tell—is surprisingly soft. Pliant encouragement meets the kiss, and Jamie feels silly for expecting anything else. Never mind the stocky strength in Sam's frame, the big hands, the powerful muscles. It's Sam's eyes Jamie should have been studying for clues, the warm affection shining there through their entire conversation in the bar. Gentleness shouldn't come as a surprise after the quiet pleasure with which Sam invited him into this room, and Jamie closes his eyes as he lets himself melt forward into impossible warmth.

There is strength enough to temper Sam's gentleness, when he finally wraps his arms around Jamie in return. Careful curiosity gives way to a more passionate exploration. Sam is the one to trace his tongue along the seam of Jamie's lips, and then to delve deeper when Jamie opens readily. Strong hands slide reverently over Jamie's body—curling at his hips, flattening along his spine, ghosting across his nape—and the low sigh Sam breathes into the kiss might be the most decadent sound Jamie has ever heard.

God, he could get used to this. He aches for more, and yet if they do nothing else tonight, he will still walk away giddy and buzzing with all the ways Sam's increasingly bold touches make him feel.

He's trembling by the time they break apart, his eyes holding stubbornly closed as he makes himself breathe, unsteady but better than no oxygen at all.

"Tell me what you need, sweetheart," Sam murmurs, touching a more fleeting kiss to the corner of Jamie's mouth, then another to his cheek, a third to the line of his jaw.

Jamie exhales, long and slow, and nuzzles in just to feel the rough brush of Sam's beard against his skin. "Can we both be more naked?"

"God yes," Sam breathes. His hands are steady when they tug at Jamie's sweater.

Jamie opens his eyes and it's not that he intends to make things more difficult, but his own efforts to undo the buttons of Sam's shirt only complicate Sam's attempt to tug *Jamie's* shirt over his head. It's an impatient scuffle, each getting in the other's way, and by the time they're both naked and tumbling together onto the bed, Jamie is barely holding back exasperated laughter.

"Anyone ever tell you you're an absolute menace?" Sam presses the words like kisses along the column of Jamie's throat, and Jamie bites down hard on his own lower lip to stifle a moan.

"Never." The word comes out more breathless than he intends, not helped by the way Sam's fingers are skimming along his hip and thigh. "I'll have you know—*fucking hell, Sam*—I'm a paragon of virtue."

"You're a paragon of something," Sam agrees, and the humor in his voice lights whole new embers in Jamie's belly.

"Do you have condoms?" he blurts. Graceless and he does not care. He's so hungry for this gorgeous man—this impossible silver fox, with all his broad muscles and soft edges—and he needs to know the shape of what they're going to do tonight.

He needs to know the exact contours of how he is allowed to touch.

"No," Sam says, but his tone is still cheerful. "Wasn't exactly planning on company tonight."

Jamie laughs—the sound is very nearly a giggle—and presses closer into the circle of powerful arms, tracing hot kisses down the side of Sam's neck, all the way to the dip at the base of his throat. "You mean reading golden age sci-fi in public isn't a deliberate seduction strategy?"

"Not usually." Sam threads deft fingers through Jamie's curls and reels him in for a longer, deeper kiss. "Can't complain about the results, though."

And god, Jamie can't complain either. Even knowing he's not going to get his mouth on Sam, or explore any of the other possibilities that condoms would open up for them, he can't bring himself to be disappointed. This is too good, perfect heat rolling through them, sliding with the clumsy enthusiasm of bodies and friction.

"Come here," Jamie growls, demanding and unapologetic as he rolls onto his back and drags Sam with him.

There's no way he could move Sam unwilling, of course. Jamie is all lithe limbs and skinny frame. He can't bring enough strength to bear to ever *make* a man built like Sam move. All that bulk and muscle could resist with almost comical ease, if they were on anything other than the same page.

But Sam takes the hint enthusiastically, covering Jamie with his own body and claiming a new and fervent kiss.

This time Jamie makes no effort to restrain his shattered groan, letting the sound resonate in his chest and convey exactly how much he is enjoying this. He arches and squirms, delighted beneath the powerful weight bearing him down into the mattress. Greedy for the easy strength with which Sam pins him in place. When Jamie spreads his legs, Sam seems to know precisely what he is asking for—precisely what he needs—because in the span of a heartbeat, a thick thigh slips into that space, shoving roughly forward and giving Jamie all the leverage he needs to rut down against firm and glorious heat.

Jamie aches to his very core. The force of arousal is making him lightheaded, his chest hot, his belly tight. He grinds down harder, moaning when Sam thrusts against him in answer.

"*Please*," Jamie gasps, and he doesn't actually know what he's asking for. *More.* Endlessly more. He is a wild contradiction—he's desperate for release—he never wants this shuddering, simple, mounting pleasure to end. His own hands wander the length of Sam's broad back, dip low, curl around a shapely ass to encourage an even more frantic pace.

"Please what?" Sam growls the question into the crook of Jamie's shoulder before nipping at his feverish skin, then soothing the spot with a kiss. "What do you need?"

Jamie wishes he knew. He wants everything at once. He's a raging wildfire of too much sensation, and he never wants to stop.

He doesn't know Sam. When they part ways, they'll probably never see each other again. How is Jamie supposed to satisfy himself with one night? One encounter? How can he possibly experience everything he craves beneath Sam's beautiful body and hands, when this is their only chance?

"*I don't know.*" He whispers the confession, rough and ragged, into the thrusting, panting quiet. "God, Sam, please just... More. Anything. *Touch me.*"

"Anything." Sam breathes the word like a benediction. "I've got you. Let me." And then his hand is slipping deftly down between their bodies, fingers curling sure and steady around Jamie's aching length.

Jamie cries out, the sound muffled in Sam's shoulder, and he arches helplessly beneath the weight pinning him to the bed. God, this *is* more. It's delicious, more perfect than the unsteady frottage of a moment before.

Sam's touch is confident and teasing, coaxing him to the precipice and then forcing him back down again, playful in the way he takes Jamie apart. The man is a virtuoso, somehow always able to tell when Jamie is too close—when orgasm is near enough to taste—and easing off just enough to prolong the exploration.

It's torture, in a way. And yet Jamie can't find the fortitude to protest. He would rather spend all night at Sam's mercy, exactly like this, than chase a quicker satisfaction that ends their unlikely intimacy.

Every instinct tells him that at the first hint of displeasure, Sam will stop toying with him and let him come—so Jamie bites his tongue and rides out the increasingly tumultuous game. He fucks into the tight circle of Sam's fist and clings to the man's enormous shoulders, savoring the answering and equally helpless panting breaths Sam growls into his ear. They are both stumbling along a perilous edge and ready to fall into oblivion.

It takes Jamie a very long time to find the coordination to touch Sam in return, but when he finally manages the trick, it's worth the effort a hundred times over. He slips his own arm down, down, down into the crush of space between their bodies. And when he finds and grips Sam's cock, the answering jolt of Sam's body on top of him—the shocky moan that rumbles from Sam's chest—is all the reward he could ever ask for.

God, how he wishes he could manage words right now. *I've got you too. Come for me.*

But he can't. His senses are too overwhelmed, his mind alight with physical pleasure that blots out all his capacity for other thoughts. He's caught up in an avalanche, and Sam is the gravity propelling him down the mountain.

Jamie comes first, but he doesn't even have time to feel bad for the way his own hand falters when orgasm cascades through him. He has just enough sense of his surroundings to feel Sam go rigid, a second messy release spilling across his hot skin, a stifled cry of pleasure buried in the line of Jamie's throat. They are both a mess, both shaking apart, and—Jamie hopes as he finally begins to drift back down—both achingly, utterly satisfied.

*

It doesn't take long, in the lingering moments that follow, for Jamie's noisy brain to interrupt what should be a boneless and uncomplicated afterglow.

He lies content in the lazy circle of Sam's arms, snuggled in close along his side. They're both still naked, cleaned up enough to be comfortable, warm despite the howling wind beyond the icy window. Lovely lethargy drifts across Jamie's tired senses, and he has no desire whatsoever to move.

That's the problem, really. He doesn't want to move, because once he does, he will have to leave. Maybe not right away, but all too soon. And he is suddenly agonizingly aware of how desperately he *does not want* to say goodbye to Sam.

All the Way Home I'll Be Warm

Jamie won't be sleeping in Sam's bed, tempting though the prospect is. For one thing, he doesn't want to impose. They both have places to be tomorrow, and if Sam's got a long drive ahead of him, he probably needs to head out just as early as Jamie does. For another, Jamie is still a little too cautious—a little too practical—to trust a complete stranger that far. Even a stranger who has burrowed so quickly past his defenses and into Jamie's heart.

It takes him a long time to grudgingly withdraw, and both he and Sam dress in a quiet that isn't nearly as awkward as it could be. Jamie doesn't complain when, clothed once more, Sam tugs him back down onto the thoroughly rumpled bed for a long, slow kiss. It feels a little too much like goodbye, but Jamie relaxes into it anyway. Savors and memorizes every detail, the hand at the small of his back, the steady heart beating below his palm, the ghost of breath across his skin when Sam finally breaks away.

It's not fair how easily this man makes Jamie's head spin.

He tries to remind himself that they don't know each other. Not really. But the admonition falls flat as he melts into Sam's arms with a wistful sigh.

When he finally opens his eyes, he finds Sam watching him with a different sort of expression. Hesitant, in a way he wasn't before. Sam looks like a man who wants to say something but is holding himself back because... Why? Considering everything they've done tonight, Jamie struggles to imagine what notion Sam can possibly be weighing to make him look so unsure.

"What's wrong?" Jamie asks without unwinding from the embrace.

"Nothing." Sam huffs a low, wry laugh. "Sorry. Just... getting tangled up in my own head. I don't want to overstep."

Jamie kisses his cheek. "You won't. Whatever it is, go ahead and ask."

Sam still pauses for a long, studious moment before asking, "Where'd you say you need to get to tomorrow? If it's not too far out of my way, maybe I could drive you."

Surprise widens Jamie's eyes, but he answers automatically. "Fergus Falls."

"I know where that is." Sam nods. "I'm following Ninety-Four the whole way through.

It wouldn't even take me off course to give you a ride."

"You'd really do that?" Jamie's not sure why he feels so shocked and incredulous at this straightforward kindness. Maybe because he had himself so wrapped up in the certainty that he's already had everything he could reasonably hope for from this man. The thought of more— even the all-too-brief reprieve of an hour in a car together—feels too good to be true. "I can't ask you for this."

"You're not asking." Sam's eyes sparkle, a glint of fondness that quickly spreads into a smile. "I'm offering. And I'm being entirely selfish. I'd love to have company for even part of my drive tomorrow. I've been traveling for days."

Jamie grins. "I know the feeling."

"That a yes?" Sam asks. "I'll understand if you'd rather not. You don't know me. And you sure as hell don't owe me anything."

"I'd love to ride with you," Jamie says. Maybe it *is* a bad idea. Maybe his sister would bury him in an hour-long lecture about making unhealthy choices like getting in cars with strangers. And hell, she'd probably be right. But Jamie can't bring himself to refuse the opportunity to keep Sam in his life just a little longer. Suddenly the prospect of going back to his own room isn't nearly as torturous, because morning will come soon enough and it will bring Sam with it.

He makes Sam exchange phone numbers preemptively, and agrees to meet him in the lobby tomorrow—early enough that Jamie hopes like hell there's decent coffee to go with the continental breakfast.

And then, giddy and energized and not at all confident he'll be able to sleep tonight, Jamie tugs Sam into one last kiss before reluctantly easing out of bed and letting himself back into the hall.

chapter four

Sam's car is a classic—a fact that Jamie recognizes even from his own dubious standpoint of knowing fuck-all about cars. It's big and boxy and completely charming, too much of a boat to be aerodynamic, with a bench seat that stretches across the entire cab and an engine that growls to life with overdramatic flare. Jamie's luggage doesn't fill even half the backseat, and the red paint job glints beneath a squintingly clear sky.

Jamie buckles in beside Sam, settling into the soft leather of the seat, savoring the unlikely heat of sunlight through ice-crusted windows.

Jamie finds his companion even more distracting in the light of day. He doesn't bother pretending not to stare at Sam's hand on the stick shift, putting the car in gear and cutting a path out onto roads that have already been plowed despite the early hour.

"So tell me about this car," Jamie says, perfectly willing to be nosy about something that doesn't skirt too close to *where is Sam going* or *where is home*. "Did you restore it yourself?"

"I bought it two weeks ago." Sam tosses Jamie a sweet, self-conscious little smile before putting his eyes quickly back on the road. "I didn't restore shit. But I haven't needed a car for a long time. Seemed worth getting the kind I've always fantasized about owning."

Jamie desperately wants to know more. *Why* hasn't Sam needed a car for so long? "Why is this car the fantasy?" he asks instead.

Sam's one-shouldered shrug is belied by a wistful expression. "My mom had one when I was a kid. Completely unreliable. It was always breaking down on us. She became a proficient mechanic just keeping up with the damn thing, but I loved that car."

Jamie studies Sam's profile through the wild pulse of fondness filling his chest. Such an impractical reason to pine after an impractical car, and he can't argue against any of it. Nostalgia is a powerful motivator.

All the Way Home I'll Be Warm

"I hope this car's been more reliable than your mom's," Jamie teases, once he finally trusts himself to sound like a normal passenger and not a smitten fool.

Sam gives an amused snort. "It's more reliable than some cars around here, anyway."

"Ouch," Jamie says, but he's grinning, wide and helpless. He can't seem to wipe the smile off his face.

An hour isn't long enough to soak up Sam's company. They talk easily the entire time—more easily than Jamie can ever remember interacting with someone so new—and as Fergus Falls looms closer, it's all he can do not to get wrapped up in his own head. God, he wishes this didn't have to be goodbye. He wishes he were brave enough to ask the more invasive questions that might give him any idea where Sam is headed, rather than holding back like a coward for fear of sabotaging something *good*.

Good things are allowed to be fleeting.

"I'm just glad to have something locked in," he says, dragging his brain back to the point he's been making for the past ten minutes. Grad school applications: the intolerable marathon. "I've got a couple friends who are still waiting to hear back from schools with wait lists, and that's... Ugh, what a nightmare."

When he glances at Sam's profile, he's not sure what to make of the pensive expression that's overtaken the man's handsome features. Some wordless intensity has lowered Sam's brow into a heavy furrow, and he's worrying his lower lip between his teeth.

"What's wrong?" Jamie asks, trying to imagine what he could possibly have said to put that look on his face.

Sam's expression clears at the question, easing by degrees, until it's wholly overwritten by the wry smile he tosses Jamie's way. The glance is fleeting, but the expression stays soft as Sam belatedly answers, "Sorry. Nothing's wrong. You're just younger than I thought you were."

Discomfort and a faint stumble of affront twist in Jamie's chest. "I'm twenty-two."

"Right." Sam glances at him again, and this time there's an edge of apology to the smile. "Like I said, nothing's wrong. I promise. Just... trying not to feel like a dirty old man. I don't want to be an asshole about something that isn't a big deal."

All the Way Home I'll Be Warm

"It's *not* a big deal. And you're not a dirty old man. I had a really good time last night." Jamie's face blazes as he says this, a complicated tangle of self-consciousness and desire twisting tight in his gut, alongside a lingering hiss of anger at the implication that he's some kid to be taken advantage of.

"So did I," Sam says, and the unmistakable warmth in his voice goes a long way toward soothing Jamie's frustration.

By the time they pull up at the curb in front of his sister's condo, any momentary strangeness has evaporated in favor of a shared reluctance to part ways. Jamie knows it's mutual, from the way Sam turns off the engine and then watches him with soul-piercing intensity. Sam's handsome face sits in a stern look now, but Jamie's not the slightest bit intimidated. He feels an answering somber weight behind his ribs. A refusal to let this be the end, even though it has to be.

"Thanks for everything," Jamie finally says when he's able to speak, and his voice comes out a little bit raspy.

"Thanks for the company." Sam watches him with a quieter smile. "You gonna be able to collect your car once they finish with it?"

"Yeah." Jamie unclicks his seatbelt and glances up the driveway. The garage door is still closed, which means Claudia and Lou haven't even started loading up the car yet. "Someone in my family should be able to drive me. Or there's always the bus."

"I wish I could offer you another ride," Sam says wistfully, "but I'll probably be busy after the holidays. I don't think I'll have an excuse to come back this direction anytime soon."

This observation makes Jamie more desperate than ever to demand some clue where Sam is ultimately going to land, but it's no more his business now than it was yesterday. Hell, what good would it do even if he knew? No matter how far along the interstate Sam's planning to travel, Jamie will be going back to the west coast at the end of January. If Sam's not going to make it even this far west anytime soon, there's no way he'll drive all the way to Spokane, Washington for...

What? A hookup? A date? A relationship they don't have?

Jamie's got no business getting this attached, this goddamn quickly, to a man he met less than twenty-four hours ago, whose last name he doesn't even know.

But if this is finally time for goodbye, then damn it, Jamie's going to make sure it's a *good one*.

He slides to the middle of the bench seat, right into Sam's personal space, and curls a hand beneath Sam's chin to tug him into a kiss. Jamie spares only the most fleeting concern over someone spotting him from the house. Even if someone sees him kissing Sam—even if they want to be judgmental—this is between Jamie and Sam and no one else. Anyone who wants to have an opinion about it can fuck right off.

Sam barely hesitates before tangling his fingers in Jamie's hair, kissing him back with a dizzying mix of wistfulness, yearning, affection. There's no suggestion of sex in this kiss, despite the passion they shared last night. It's a goodbye. Both of them grasping at one last fleeting connection before Jamie has to get out of the car.

"Text me, okay?" Jamie says breathlessly when Sam reluctantly pushes him away. "Please? Whenever you get to your friend's house? I want to know you made it in one piece."

"I will," Sam vows, then kisses him once more. Quick and hard this time, and so desperate that it takes every scrap of Jamie's willpower just to get out of the car. He drags his luggage from the backseat with a helpless twinge of loss, hating the finality of the sound as he slams the door shut and backs all the way onto the sidewalk.

He waves goodbye and waits as Sam pulls away down the street, watching the car disappear through a cloudy dusting of snow.

*

The second he sets foot in the house—using the key his sister gave him almost the second the mortgage papers were signed—Jamie gets confirmation that no one cares who he was just kissing. No one even noticed the car pull up.

Lou and little May are both in the kitchen, ostensibly eating breakfast. Lou is mostly ignoring the bagel on her plate in favor of a full mug of coffee, her narrow-eyed expression thick with sleep, her mouse-brown hair a wispy mess not yet combed through. Her lovely face looks like she'd just as soon crawl right back into bed, and Jamie wonders how early May woke the grownups this morning. Ever since switching from a crib to a normal bed, there's no stopping the world's smallest Morning Person from wreaking havoc on her moms.

May, by contrast, looks sunny and alert in her highchair, making absolute carnage of a bowl of fruit and oatmeal.

"Morning, Lou," Jamie says, and leans over to very carefully plant a kiss to the crown of May's head—the only part of his niece not sticky with smeared fruit.

Lou grunts an acknowledgment and sips more coffee. Jamie doesn't take the lack of enthusiasm personally. He and Lou get along just fine—and he knows her well enough to recognize there's no chance of a more human interaction at this hour.

"Uncle Jamie!" May squeaks, brandishing a plastic spoon at him. The syllables come out sounding more like *Un-ka SHAY-mee!*, thanks partly to the faint toddler clumsiness that still muddles most of her words, and partly to the fact that her mouth is full of oatmeal and blueberries.

"Morning to you too, goofball." He heads for the coffee pot himself, ready for a *good* cup of coffee after the uninspired sludge from the hotel lobby. Without taking his eyes off the cupboard full of clean mugs, he asks, "Claudia up yet?"

"Claudia's right here," his sister announces, swooping into the kitchen and squashing him into a hug. She is an inescapable force, despite standing several inches shorter than him, and she sounds exasperated when she asks, "How did you get here so fast? I thought I was picking you up from the bus station. I've been waiting for you to call with an eta."

It's too early for lectures on accepting rides from strangers, so Jamie answers honestly but with key information absent. "A friend gave me a ride. Need help loading the car?"

"Not yet." Claudia waves him off. "Soon, I guess. If we hit the road before Lou's caffeinated, the road rage might put us all in an early grave."

"You could just *not let her drive*," Jamie points out.

"I heard that," Lou retorts from the other end of the kitchen.

All the Way Home I'll Be Warm

It's several hours later before they hit the road, Jamie riding in the backseat beside May for the first leg of the journey. He dozes for the better part of an hour, and his dreams are disoriented but pleasant. Quiet heat. Warm smiles. When he wakes to the same snow-covered fields he dozed off to, he finds himself achingly aware of how much he already misses Sam. Unreasonable maybe, to have gotten so attached so quickly. But he feels it just the same.

He jumps at the chance to switch spots when Lou and Claudia trade off driving. The front passenger seat is heated, for one thing, and Jamie is chilly despite his thick jacket and the steady heat pouring out from the vents. More importantly, he barely gets to talk to his sister lately, between his busy school schedule and her whole working-full-time-while-raising-a-three-year-old thing.

"Has Dad told you more about Victor's visit?" Claudia asks, as they pull from the rest area ramp back onto eastbound Ninety-Four.

"No." Jamie had almost managed to forget his consternation over the prospect of living side-by-side with his dad's mysterious friend. "I mean, sounds like it'll be a long visit. But I already figured on that part. Do *you* know anything about this guy?"

"Sure. I know he's been Dad's best friend for literal decades, and he's staying in Saint Paul until he figures out where to settle down." There's a cheeky air to this delivery—Claudia knows damn well she's not offering new or useful information—and she still sounds impish when she adds, "He's a little behind on having a life after twenty years away."

"Twenty years away *where?*" Jamie doesn't bother to conceal his exasperation. He's been too busy to ask their dad this question, and maybe a little embarrassed that it never occurred to him to wonder before. It's just that Victor Leone has been a non-entity Jamie's entire life. His existence is pure story and myth and the occasional fond smile on Warren Phipps's face. It never occurred to Jamie to wonder where he actually was.

"Antarctica," Claudia says without missing a beat.

Jamie scowls. "You don't have to be a brat about it. I was asking a serious question."

"It was a serious answer. Vic went to Antarctica for work. He's been there ever since."

"For *twenty years*?" Jamie stares at his sister's profile, but Claudia looks completely sincere. "Doing what? And who spends twenty straight years in Antarctica?"

"Plenty of people, I'd imagine." Claudia shrugs one shoulder. "And I'm sure he got to take vacations and stuff."

"Yeah, but… Antarctica? Why?"

"I don't actually know what he was doing there. Top secret science stuff for some government agency."

"Sure." Jamie rolls his eyes. "Go ahead, pull the other one."

"No, really." Claudia hits the turn signal and then merges into the passing lane. "I mean, okay, it's not actually top secret. Something to do with biochemistry probably? It's not like I grilled Dad about his CV." This time Claudia's shrug uses both shoulders, as if to more thoroughly encompass the sentiment, *I have no fucking idea*.

Jamie breathes a considering hum. "I wonder what he's like."

"Don't you remember him? We met him a few times when we were kids."

"We absolutely did not." Surely Jamie would remember. Warren and Anika Phipps share a wide and eclectic social circle, and Jamie's got a good memory for his parents' friends, most of whom are some combination of sweet and strange and weirdly ambitious. But he's got no memory whatsoever of Victor Leone.

Claudia seems to consider this protest with an uncharacteristic lack of argument, before answering, "You might only have met him once. Right before he left for Antarctica. And you would've been tiny."

That makes more sense. "What do *you* remember about him?"

"I mean, I was just a kid too. But I remember him being really nice. Like, all these parties full of grown-ups who were too wrapped up in each other to play with me, and Mom and Dad were both obviously busy. *You* were just a boring baby. But Vic would build snowmen with me, or play hide and seek, or drag some of the other grown-ups into my stupid fake tea parties." A nostalgic smile twitches at one corner of her mouth. "I was sad when I found out he was moving a zillion miles away."

All the Way Home I'll Be Warm

"It's going to be weird, living with this dude for a month when we've never met. Do you think I'll have to share my bathroom?"

Claudia laughs. "You will absolutely have to share your bathroom."

Jamie is saved from coming up with a pithy retort by a buzz from his phone.

He fishes it from his pocket and finds a text from Sam waiting for him.

I lived.

Jamie grins, hopefully not looking like too much of a smitten doofus, and sends off a quick reply. *Good. How was the drive?*

Several seconds pass, the animated ellipsis telling him Sam is still typing, before the answer finally comes through. *Long and boring. Wish I could've kept you the whole way.*

A pulse of longing fills Jamie's chest as he dashes off one more reply. *Would've been fun. Maybe next time.* He feels bold and wistful all at once, and maybe even hopeful that this isn't just wishful thinking after all. He smiles even wider when Sam immediately sends back a ridiculous sequence of emojis: a red car, a grinning face, a thumbs up.

Never mind the question of whether it's realistic to hope he'll see Sam again. For the moment, it's enough knowing Sam likes the idea.

When Jamie puts his phone away, his sister is so pointedly not watching him that it's impossible to ignore the weight of her attention. Her brow has arched high towards her curly hairline, and a glint of curiosity flashes in her profile.

"Do not start," Jamie grouses, but he's still too delighted to shake the sappy grin off his face.

"I didn't say a word."

*

They reach their destination just after four, following a bumpy journey that involved stopping at every rest area between Fergus Falls and Saint Paul. Jamie doesn't mind. It's still faster than he would've reached the Cities on a bus, and significantly less stressful.

Warren and Anika Phipps have outdone themselves with the holiday decor. Jamie knew it was coming—his parents both separately sent him photos of the light-bedecked facade of their house—and yet seeing the display in person is about fifty times more alarming. They haven't gone in for any inflatable trees or snowmen, but the giant metal-frame Santa, complete with sleigh and reindeer, is a sight to behold even in daylight.

Sunset hasn't quite had time to roll through and swathe the horizon in darkness yet, but the lights are on anyway. Intricate cascades along the eaves are just the beginning, complemented by glowing green wreaths along the blue walls of the house, and white strings of light limning every window frame. The two enormous pine trees at opposite edges of the front yard haven't escaped either. They stand draped in matching overloads of string lights, the bulbs glinting in rainbow colors that render the evening's cloudy dusk aggressively cheerful.

Even the walkway between curb and front porch has been adorned with a temporary railing of swooping lights to mark out the way.

All of this is familiar, if a bit much. And if it weren't for the single unknown factor of the visitor, probably already waiting inside, Jamie would be perfectly at ease as Lou pulls up to the curb. He finds himself on edge over the notion of sharing space with a stranger, even though he's got no rational reason to be nervous. Maybe it's just that this is someone who means so much to his parents—or at least to his dad—and Jamie's always been the sort of guy to stress over making a good first impression.

And maybe he's overthinking things. But if he knew how to cut off *that* habit, he'd have done it years ago.

They park in front of the house, rather than following the big winding driveway around back, and Claudia immediately hands a big saran-wrapped bowl to Jamie between the seats.

"Here," she says. "Carry this."

He glances down and finds it full almost to bursting with buckeyes. Not the actual nut, but the hand-crafted balls of peanut butter and chocolate that so closely resemble the items found in nature. They're probably intended for the big Christmas Eve dinner Warren and Anika always insist on hosting. This is far too many sweets to consume in the span of a short visit otherwise.

Jamie holds the bowl on his lap while Lou and Claudia fuss with luggage and toddler. He takes a moment to pull out his phone and send a self-indulgent text to Sam.

Time to be aggressively sociable around some dude I've never met before, pray for me.

Sam texts back with heartening speed. *You seemed pretty good at it last night.*

Jamie barely stifles a laugh as he shoots back, *You were a special case. Also flirting with my dad's best friend would be a disastrous way to break the ice.*

Then the car doors finally start to open around him, letting in brutal gusts of wind—so Jamie pockets his phone, hoists the perilously over-stuffed bowl of buckeyes in one arm, shoulders his backpack, and follows his sister into the house.

Anika Phipps already stands in the mudroom, poised to demand hugs before anyone has a chance to set down their burdens—scooping little May up into her arms last of all, for a noisy and squirming embrace. Warren hovers in the door at the edge of the tiny hallway, his attention somewhere behind him as he tosses a laughing command over his shoulder.

"Vic, c'mon man, they're here! Stop grinning at your phone, and come meet my offspring!"

Jamie has just enough time to give his dad a one-armed hug before Victor Leone steps around the corner.

The sight of *Sam* standing there, real and gorgeous and unmistakable, hits Jamie squarely in the chest, and he fumbles the bowl of buckeyes.

He's vaguely aware of his sister shouting his name as the bowl falls. Impact snaps the saran wrap, scattering sweets across the floor in all directions. The instant cascade of candy distracts Jamie's family, as everyone scrambles after the carnage, apparently oblivious to the shock that sent the bowl tumbling from his hands in the first place.

But Jamie stands perfectly still.

And across the entry hall, eyes wide with an incredulity to match his own, Sam—

—*Victor*—

—does the same.

chapter five

Jamie recovers first, or at least manages to get himself moving to help corral escaped candy. His head is still spinning, too stunned to process this impossible new information, but some instinctive autopilot has kicked in and turned him back into a functioning human.

More or less.

He's acutely aware of Victor belatedly joining the fray, though at this point the rescue attempt is hopeless. The mudroom floor is nowhere near clean enough to salvage fallen food, and only two buckeyes have managed to stay inside the bowl. Jamie would feel guilty for being the reason so much time and effort have gone to waste, if he weren't so busy reeling for completely different reasons.

At least everyone seems inclined to laugh off the disaster instead of getting angry at him. Whether it's because everyone's still caught up in more jovial spirits—or because May is so damn cute in her unsuccessful efforts to eat the candies before the adults can pry them out of her hands—the overall mood stays cheerful.

Somewhere along the way, someone gives May the two sweets that didn't land on the floor, and by the time they're gone her face and hands are smeared with chocolate.

"Don't worry about it, Jamie." Claudia says the words just for him, under her breath and soft with laughter. She gives his shoulder a squeeze as Lou and Warren pile the last of the fallen buckeyes back into the bowl. "Plenty of time to make more before Christmas Eve."

"Yeah." Jamie wipes his hands on his jeans and pushes to his feet. "Still. I'm sorry. I'll go buy the stuff tomorrow."

He barely registers that Warren is speaking, as his dad first introduces the chocolate-bedecked three-year-old, then adds, "My daughter Claudia, and her lovely wife Lou."

All the Way Home I'll Be Warm

Jamie's heart gives a noticeable stumble when everyone's attention shifts to him and Warren says, "This is my son, Jamie."

His breath catches in his throat and he freezes again, wondering how Victor is going to respond. Surely Jamie's heart is racing so loud the whole neighborhood can hear it. Surely their mutual mortification will tip everyone off that something has gone awry.

Then Victor smiles, and the expression seems honest, if a little strained.

"Glad to meet you, Jamie. I hope we can be friends." Victor's grip is strong when Jamie accepts the man's offered handshake. He meets those drowning-deep eyes and wonders if anyone else notices the way Victor's voice hitches on the word 'friends'.

Victor. Not Sam. Jamie's brain catches and spins out, and he suddenly can't decide whether he feels more betrayed or confused through the stunned haze. What the hell is he going to do?

There's no chance to hold the handshake too long, even if Jamie wanted to, since everyone quickly bursts back into motion. There's still a car full of gifts and luggage to unpack, rooms to settle into, a cozy dinner to prepare. Jamie leaves his own bags at the base of the stairs in favor of helping unload Claudia's car—swapping out to entertain May for a while when it's time for the heaviest items that are quite frankly not his problem. He'd rather play with a three-year-old anyway, and considering how long it's been since he saw her in person rather than through a phone or computer screen, he's heartened at how quickly she warms to chasing him around the living room.

The whole house is exactly as noisy and chaotic as Jamie needs to distract himself from the disbelieving maelstrom of his thoughts. Buried at the core of the storm is a disappointment he does not dare examine. It's a little too close to heartbreak, and Jamie refuses to be heartbroken over a man he met *yesterday* and had no reasonable expectation of ever seeing again. The fact that Sam is Victor—is Warren Phipps's longtime best friend—shouldn't change anything.

But god damn it, it does. Instead of spending the evening sending flirtatious texts to a gorgeous stranger who's vanished to fuck knows where, Jamie has to watch Victor from across the room, knowing there won't be a repeat of the intimacy they shared last night.

With all the energetic disorder of the evening, dinner doesn't happen until almost eight o'clock. Even this is chaotic, albeit an order of magnitude less so than the hours leading up to it. May refuses to remain at the table, having already been fed at a more reasonable hour, which leaves the adults—including Victor—taking turns away from their own dinners to distract her, so that everyone else can eat in peace. By the time everyone manages to finish, it's later still. Past nine o'clock, and Claudia's upstairs trying to get a fussy and overstimulated three-year-old to sleep, while everyone else helps clear the table and pack up leftovers.

Jamie runs away the second the last plate is clean and dry, clumsily turning down Anika's offer to heat up some cider if people want to go sit by the fireplace. She looks at him with startled curiosity.

"Too much driving," he says, before she can start reading god-knows-what into his expression. "If I get anywhere near that fireplace, I'll fall asleep for sure."

"You know we wouldn't be offended, love."

"Yeah." He gives her a cautious smile, and then a more decisive hug. "But I'd rather be in pajamas and a warm bed. I'll see you in the morning, okay?" It's the most dishonest thing he's said to her in years. Jamie has no intention of changing into pajamas. There's too much restless energy beneath his skin. He can't imagine sitting still in his parents' company right now, no matter how delighted he is to see them. All he wants—to a disorienting and powerful degree—is to talk to Victor Leone. Alone. And if he can't have that, he needs to hide himself away and build his defenses up, so that he's better equipped to face tomorrow without giving the entire game away.

He hugs his dad too, and then Lou on his way toward the stairs. Claudia still hasn't emerged from doing battle with May's bedtime, and Victor has disappeared somewhere, saving Jamie from the quandary of what might constitute an appropriate goodnight for a man his family doesn't know he slept with.

Jamie's bags are gone from the base of the stairs, and he's not surprised to step into his old room and discover someone has deposited them just inside the door. The space has been redecorated over the past couple years, making it a pleasant but generic guest room, and for this Jamie is genuinely grateful. Any nostalgia he might harbor is undercut by how strange he feels in his own skin. He doesn't think he could cope with returning to his childhood bedroom, when his entire brain is caught and repeatedly tripping over the contradiction between Victor Leone's presence and the things Jamie wants to do to him.

Better like this, an almost anonymous space that's more like a fancy bed-and-breakfast than a reminder of being a kid. The blue walls have been painted over with a pale moss green, and all the oak furniture complements the color, even the narrow bed with its deep emerald comforter. The carpet is long gone, revealing smooth wooden flooring several shades lighter than the bureau and bedposts, and the old window—looking out across a wide backyard— has been replaced to keep out the draft.

It's an inviting space. And Jamie doesn't know what to do with himself now that he's standing in it.

He unpacks his clothing into the enormous bureau, settling in for a long stay. He lays out his softest pair of pajamas, but doesn't change into them. Even after sneaking across the hall to brush his teeth, he doesn't undress when he returns. Soon everyone else will turn in, and he's ready. Waiting. Listening for the sound of footsteps in the hall, to tell him when Victor has finally come upstairs, because Jamie is fully prepared to knock on his door and demand some answers.

Lou shuffles past first, her bare feet quiet on the steps—just below Jamie's door—and on the wood-paneled hallway disappearing to the opposite end of the house. Claudia must've texted her the all-clear after finally getting May to sleep. Then, after an eon, a heavier tread of footsteps climbs the stairs.

That can only be Victor. Neither of Jamie's parents has any reason to come upstairs tonight, when the master bedroom is on the ground floor at the back of the house. Which means Jamie's racing heart finally has something to focus on, as he listens to the steady progress and waits for Victor's steps to vanish into the second guest room along the hall.

All the Way Home I'll Be Warm

But the heavy footsteps stop directly in front of Jamie's door. And he has just enough time to brace himself before a soft rap of knuckles breaks the impatient quiet.

Jamie crosses the room in an instant, opening the door to let Victor hurry inside, closing it again with a click.

There's restlessness in the way Victor strides across the room, as though trying to put a respectable distance between himself and Jamie. Gone is the calm facade he's worn all evening, replaced by tension in those broad shoulders and a visible clench of his jaw. He stands by the window without bothering to glance out at the moonlit ice and snow in the yard below.

Jamie doesn't want to admit how reassuring it is to see Victor like this. Unsteady. Unsure. Every bit as off-balance as Jamie has felt since arriving home.

"I'm so sorry, Jamie. I swear I had no idea." Victor's voice rumbles with feeling, and it's obvious he's trying to keep his voice down for the sake of discretion. He stares at Jamie with an expression that could mean so many things. Disbelief, guilt, horror, disappointment. Maybe all those things and more, and Jamie's heart threatens to break all over again.

He doesn't want Victor to feel guilty about being with him.

Jamie's not sure what alternative he can offer. He's certainly been entertaining his own cycle of panic since realizing who Victor is. But he can't bring himself to regret last night, no matter how awkward and strange it all seems in retrospect.

Mostly, he realizes with a shaky jolt, he just wants Victor to *not be Warren's best friend.* That would be a fantastic place to start.

Jamie belatedly takes his hand off the doorknob, but he keeps to his side of the room. Selfish instinct urges him to follow Victor and eradicate this unwelcome gulf between them. But he doesn't dare. His hands still want too desperately to reach out and hold on. Better to stay right where he is.

"You said your name was *Sam*!" Jamie hisses, barely above a whisper.

"There were three Victors on base, including me. I started going by my middle name almost a decade ago. I swear I wasn't trying to con you." Victor offers a helpless shrug, hands open at his sides. "I just didn't think about it."

The simplicity of this reasoning takes the wind out of Jamie's sails, and for a long moment he just stands there absorbing the information. Only as the anger melts away does he register just how hurt he was at the thought of Sam— Victor—lying to him last night. It's a powerful relief, to realize it was a careless misunderstanding and not a conscious deception, even if the rest of their situation remains an unmitigated disaster.

"Do you… want me to keep calling you Sam?" Jamie asks carefully.

Victor's shoulders slump. "No. I need to get used to Victor again. It's my name, I always meant to reclaim it eventually." His mouth twitches down at one corner, a pained little twist as he adds, "Besides, if you start calling me Sam, your folks will ask why. I don't think that's a conversation we want to have."

Jamie flinches at the notion. "No. Definitely not."

"I'm sorry," Victor says softly. "I planned to stay in touch, but I sure as hell didn't intend for it to happen like this."

The words draw Jamie a halting step forward. "You planned to stay in touch?"

This shouldn't surprise him. They exchanged phone numbers. They've texted each other multiple times today. Before he walked into his parents' house, Jamie was starting to genuinely hope there was some chance of keeping Sam in his life, distance be damned. He shouldn't be this relieved to learn Victor was thinking the same.

As though somehow following this careening mess of thoughts, Victor's expression shifts and he says, "Of course I planned to stay in touch. Only a fool lets go of a good thing without fighting for it."

A good thing. Jamie's stomach flips, and his chest twists tight and hot. He hates this. He hates that Victor is right. They had a good thing, and it doesn't matter. How are they supposed to fight for any piece of this, now that they know the truth?

They can't. That's the shitty and relentless reality of their situation. They can't have this.

"I know," Victor agrees miserably, deciphering Jamie's glower.

All the Way Home I'll Be Warm

"This sucks," Jamie says. God, he can't even bring himself to wish it hadn't happened. Maybe it would be less torturous if he didn't know what he was losing, but he can't stand the thought of never having Victor at all.

"Yeah." Victor swallows hard and wrenches his gaze away, breaking eye contact with a jolt that feels like it could shatter them both. "I'm sorry. I wish…"

"Me too." Jamie hates that this is where they have to leave things, but he's not going to beg for something that will put Victor in an impossible position. Any connection between them—any revisiting of the intimacy they shared last night—would fuck things up with his dad for sure. It would be messy and complicated at best, and there's no way Jamie's family would understand. Feelings would be hurt. Friendships would be devastated, maybe beyond repair.

One night of sex—even really good sex— can't be worth that kind of collateral damage.

A yearning ache burns in the stillness between them. Jamie shivers and lets his gaze drift to the floor. He needs to let this go. He *will* let this go. But the disappointment hurts just the same.

It's Victor who stirs first from their silent impasse, and he moves past Jamie with reluctant steps. Sets his hand to the door without actually turning the knob. Hesitates there, almost within reach.

"Hey," Jamie says. He draws a steadying breath and eases closer. "It was nice. You don't have to be sorry about last night."

Then, emboldened by the way Victor sways toward him instead of away, Jamie leans in and kisses him on the cheek. If the kiss lingers a little longer than is strictly decent, so what? No one's here to call them out. Jamie needs this, if he has any hope of treating this conversation like a goodbye.

Yes, Victor will be living in the room immediately next-door to Jamie's. Yes, they'll be cohabiting for a full month, until Jamie goes back to Spokane, or Victor sorts out the housing market, whichever comes first. But starting over as strangers will mean a whole different landscape to the path that brought them here. Jamie is not allowed to want Victor. If he's going to have any hope of moving on, of retroactively sorting this gorgeous man into a box labeled *Off*

Limits, then first he needs to acknowledge the fleeting intimacy they've already shared.

Jamie inhales sharply when Victor catches his hand and presses a kiss to his palm. Quick and rueful and over far too soon.

By the time Jamie gathers himself, Victor has already vanished into the hall—closing the door between them and leaving Jamie bereft.

chapter six

The next day would be torment enough, figuring out how to coexist absent any reasonable expectations beyond friendship. But it's two days until Christmas, and the first thing Jamie sees when he stumbles downstairs is Victor Leone sitting on the couch beside the as-yet-undecorated Christmas tree.

Rumpled and soft.

Reading holiday-themed storybooks to May.

There's a mug on the end table, and more than once as Jamie stands there, Victor manages to deftly take a sip without spilling coffee on either book or three-year-old, despite May wriggling all over the couch.

At one point, May tries to reach for the mug, and Jamie's impressed at how easily Victor quells her by simply raising an eyebrow and lifting the coffee out of reach.

Jamie can't remember ever winning a clash of wills with May so quickly. He wonders what sorcery is involved, and if maybe Victor can give him some tips on how to convince a toddler to respect him.

Sounds of activity echo from the kitchen, but Jamie can't tell who else is awake. It's still dark outside, despite the cheerful ambiance of the living room, and Jamie's not the only person in this house who begrudges mornings. Here before him, he watches Victor read the final page of some book about a little monster who wants to be a reindeer, and then May pronounces a shrill, "All done!" and tosses the book aside.

"Done reading?" Victor asks, laughter rumbling through the question.

"No." May scrambles down from the couch and collects another book from a small mountain of them balanced precariously on the coffee table at the center of the room. "This one."

Then she's back to the couch, handing the book over so that she can manage the clumsy climbing feat necessary to reclaim her place on the high cushions. Victor doesn't try to help, which means he's been paying attention. May always insists on doing things herself, and this morning is no exception, as she finally regains her equilibrium and burrows in beneath Victor's arm to open the book.

The sight is too adorable to tolerate, not helped at all by the fact that Victor is wearing flannel pajamas in a grid of red and green, and they're a close match for May's footed onesie with its pattern of Christmas trees. Victor's hair is disheveled, his posture relaxed. He looks barely awake, and achingly sweet.

Jamie braces himself for an extra heartbeat, then strides forward into the room.

"Merry Christmas, Uncle Jamie!" May says before Victor manages to begin reading the new book.

"Not Christmas yet, goofball." Jamie grins despite the conflicted twist in his chest.

"Tomorrow?"

"Day after that." Jamie drops to the floor, kneeling beside the tree and opening his arms wide. "Do I get a hug?"

"Oh!" May climbs off the couch and hurls herself into his arms so fast that, if Jamie weren't braced for impact, they would both topple over into the tree. Her little arms wrap around his neck tight enough to choke the breath out of him, but Jamie doesn't complain. He's busy scooping her into a fierce hug and rising to his feet—a maneuver that makes him abruptly aware just how much bigger she's gotten since the last time he did this—and giving her a dizzying spin.

"Your moms helping in the kitchen?" he asks, halting the disorienting momentum and settling May more securely on his hip.

"No," May announces primly, like Jamie has just asked the silliest question of all time. "They're sleeping. They said, ask someone else to read stories."

Jamie snorts, amusement shimmering like an extra layer of glitter over the affection in his chest. "Of course they did." And then, because he can't spend the rest of December and all of January not acknowledging the man, he faces the couch and lets his smile turn wry. "Morning, Vic."

All the Way Home I'll Be Warm

It feels a little weird to use the nickname, but then, it's not like calling him *Victor* feels especially normal after so memorably meeting *Sam*. Victor's answering smile is soft and yet somehow feels like a conspiracy. A shared secret. Jamie sets May on the floor as his face heats, doing his best to pretend there's nothing out of the ordinary happening here.

"You sleep okay?" Victor asks, looking Jamie over with an assessing eye.

"Not really," Jamie admits, and this feels like a secret too. Like he's admitting something he shouldn't. Like he's calling Victor to attention when he should let the strangeness between them lie undisturbed. But May is already climbing back onto the couch and demanding Victor's focus, and the moment passes as quickly as her next demand that Victor start reading.

"Coffee," Jamie announces, and makes his way into the kitchen, desperate for caffeine and distraction, for once grateful when his dad puts him immediately to work mixing cookie dough.

It's not long before Claudia trudges into the kitchen—alone, because there's no way Lou will be out of bed before ten o'clock—and makes a beeline straight for the coffee pot. She joins the conversation Anika and Warren have been trying unsuccessfully to draw Jamie into, and he can't even bring himself to feel guilty for having no idea what they're talking about. He's still too wrapped up in his own head, resisting the urge to duck back into the living room just to see what book May and Victor are reading now.

Resisting the urge to snuggle right in with them, for reasons that have nothing to do with a lazy morning, and everything to do with a closeness he is not allowed to crave from Victor Leone.

"Warren, darling, I thought you said you bought extra rolled oats." Anika's voice is accompanied by the thud of multiple cupboards shutting in sequence.

"I did," Warren says. "Look under the— No. Wait. I think they're still in my car." Jamie watches them both disappear toward the garage and doesn't bother calling out that it doesn't take two people to carry a container of dry oatmeal. There's no point trying to dissuade Anika and Warren Phipps from their rhythms and routines—and if sometimes it seems like they're two people sharing a single brain, there is something sweet in how perfectly in-step they are after thirty years of marriage.

The kitchen goes suddenly quiet with their departure. Jamie tries to return his attention to the cookie dough beneath his rolling pin, but a prickle at his nape makes him turn around instead.

He finds Claudia watching him with an expression she would never admit is concern. Her hair has been tugged back into a high ponytail, her pajamas covered with a fluffy red bathrobe. She looks like she could crawl right back into bed and fall asleep, and yet there's something alert and serious in her eyes.

"You okay?" She leans a hip on the nearest counter. "You're not usually this quiet."

"Of course I'm okay."

"You haven't eaten any of the cookie dough."

"Maybe I'm trying not to get salmonella." Humor tinges the words, and the smile Jamie finally manages is an honest one.

"When has that ever stopped you?" Claudia retorts, but she's stopped giving off that faintly worried vibe. A moment later, when she refills her coffee mug and heads into the living room to make sure her child hasn't set anything on fire, the silence—fleeting though it is—finally allows Jamie to breathe.

*

They decorate the tree right after lunch, a process rendered chaotic by May's insistence on helping.

Even with carefully modulated access to only the least breakable ornaments, more of them land on the ground than stay amid the branches. When she eventually concedes to let the adults help her loop finicky strings around branches, they make better progress. The nearly random collection of baubles, reindeer, candy canes, and miniature sleds still clusters mostly at the bottom of the tree, until there are no more free branches within May's reach.

Everyone else has been hanging more breakable decorations amid higher branches, but the result is hilariously lopsided.

"It's a bit of a disaster, isn't it?" Anika murmurs, a quiet aside that only Jamie hears.

He laughs and says, "May, c'mere." Then hoists her into his arms when she scampers close, and holds her up to reach a higher branch for the gaudy red caboose-shaped ornament she's been trying to hang.

It's not a perfect strategy. For one thing, Jamie's arms get tired long before May is ready to be finished with this exciting new venture. For another, they end up dropping ornaments on the floor far more often than not. But it's worth it, for the way May giggles, and for the smile on his sister's face, and even for the not-so-sneaky photo Anika snaps when she thinks Jamie isn't paying attention.

Jamie isn't normally a fan of having his picture taken, but he's going to ask his mom to text him this one instead of making her delete it.

When he finally puts May down, the tree looks fractionally more balanced and there are only a few more ornaments left to hang. Lou takes up the challenge of hoisting her daughter for the home stretch, and Jamie gratefully retreats.

There are plenty of places he could sit. Warren and Anika Phipps entertain often, and their living room is packed with an unreasonable amount of comfortable furniture. But the couch is closest, and even if it weren't,

Victor sits at one end of it looking thoughtful. His glance darts away, as though he's been watching Jamie and doesn't want to get caught.

Jamie can't even bring himself to mind. And when he collapses beside Victor, the sudden proximity ignites his senses.

It's not that he's sitting inappropriately close. He's claimed the middle cushion, avoiding the spot Lou just vacated in what he hopes will look like polite deference to not stealing his sister-in-law's seat. But Victor's arm is draped across the back of the couch, and Jamie's slouch results in an unanticipated moment of contact. It's all he can do not to give a physical jolt at what feels like a torrent of electric heat along his spine. Victor's arm tenses at his back, but the touch doesn't withdraw.

And when Jamie doesn't retreat either— when he exchanges a surreptitious glance with Victor and then quickly looks away—the stillness that settles between them is the best torture Jamie's ever felt.

"About those buckeyes," Claudia says, when the tree is truly complete and all the boxes have been tidied away into the crawl space beneath the stairs.

All the Way Home I'll Be Warm

Jamie pops up from the couch, trying very hard not to look guilty—or at the very least, hoping if he *does* look guilty, people will ascribe the reaction to how bad he still feels about ruining an entire batch of candy—and says, "I can go buy the replacement supplies."

Warren laughs outright at this. "You think we don't have peanut butter, powdered sugar and melting chocolate?"

"In abundance," Anika adds, from her place on the floor amid the blocks May has begun stacking into perilous configurations. They're not actually blocks meant for playing. They spell out MERRY CHRISTMAS when assembled together on the mantlepiece. But Jamie's sure as hell not going to suggest that building towers is an unworthy use for them.

"Okay, then I'll... start melting chocolate, I guess?"

"I wasn't actually going to demand you do it yourself," Claudia says, but the glint in her eyes belies the protest. And Jamie can't exactly blame her for not wanting to repeat the time-consuming activity.

"It's fine. My fault it needs doing in the first place, it might as well be me." He gives a shrug.

"Besides, it's not baking. I shouldn't be able to mess it up too bad."

"Now I *definitely* don't want you doing it by yourself," Claudia says.

"I'll help him." Victor's gruff baritone sends a shiver the entire length of Jamie's spine.

And it's fine. It's normal. It's perfectly okay. No one gives them any strange looks as they leave the living room together and make their silent way into the kitchen.

Jamie's a little nervous the quiet will linger between them, unbreakable without addressing the things they absolutely cannot say out loud where there's so much chance of being overheard. But searching for everything they'll need, the correct kitchenware, the necessary ingredients, shatters the tension into more manageable shards. It still feels like something of a minefield, but Jamie can handle this, especially once he divides his attention between Victor and the task at hand.

In the end, they look up a recipe, because neither Jamie nor Victor actually knows how to make buckeyes. Jamie's already upended the pieces of chocolate into a glass bowl when Victor—staring at his phone screen—says,

All the Way Home I'll Be Warm

"Wait. Don't melt the chocolate yet. We need to make and chill the peanut butter balls first."

They also, it turns out, need more than just peanut butter, sugar and chocolate.

But a second round of supply gathering goes just as well as the first. And after using the mixer to make quick work of beating everything together, it's right on to rolling walnut-sized balls of peanut butter onto trays covered in wax paper. Tedious work, and yet Jamie can't bring himself to mind this excuse to have Victor entirely to himself.

Even if they do have to resist certain conversational topics. Even if the urge to flirt is almost overwhelming. Even if every question and answer feels like it's in code, and Jamie has lost the decryption software. The questions Victor asks him while they work—about school, about Washington, about the duration of Jamie's winter break—are wholly innocuous, and yet there's a shared intensity running like an undercurrent beneath every word they exchange.

"I don't usually stay in Minnesota all the way through January," Jamie admits, slipping another tray into an already overfull fridge. "I always took a J-term class. But not this year."

"Needed a break?"

Jamie huffs a laugh. "Understatement of the decade. My whole fall semester's been senior seminars and advanced lab work."

"I know what that's like." Victor considers his current ball of peanut butter and apparently deems it unworthy, adding more filling and forming it once more into a little sphere more perfect than any of Jamie's creations.

Jamie watches him work for a while, mesmerized by the elegant strength in Victor's hands. Painfully aware that he's being too obvious. Utterly unable to stop.

"Anyway," he finally says, when he scrounges his voice back from the depths of distraction, "I've already confirmed my spot with the grad program I want. I figure that means I deserve a January off, for once in my goddamn life." It's not like he's going to be able to get away much once he starts his master's program. Even summers are going to be tricky, if he wants to start squeezing in internships and work experience for his chosen area of study.

All the Way Home I'll Be Warm

"I wanted to ask what you were studying," Victor says, low-voiced, keeping his eyes on his hands while he works. "Before, I mean. During our drive, when you were telling me about applying to grad school. But I didn't want to pry about specifics when... Y'know..."

Jamie huffs an exasperated laugh, and he keeps his voice equally low. "You're completely ridiculous. I would've been happy to tell you." Then again, if their conversation had dipped into anything as specific as geography or programs of study, Victor might have connected the dots sooner. Jamie knows how proud his parents are of his academic achievements and his grad school plans. There's no chance in hell Warren hasn't talked Victor's ear off, about Jamie accepting an offer from the Spokane campus's master's program for Speech and Hearing Sciences. Surely it would have been one coincidence too many.

Victor has finished sculpting the last of the peanut butter and is watching Jamie now. He looks every bit as conflicted as Jamie feels—as though his mind has wandered down the same troublesome avenue—and Jamie swallows hard, giving himself a firm mental shake.

"What about you?" He forces himself to step away from the counter under the pretext of finding the abandoned bowl of chocolate waiting to be melted. It's still too soon to put the damn thing in the microwave—the peanut butter balls need to chill for twenty minutes— but at least it gives Jamie something to do with his hands.

"I... don't have any plans that involve school," Victor says. He sounds sincerely perplexed.

"No, I just meant... What do you want to do next, now that you're here? Dad said you'll probably be staying a couple months at least."

"Oh." Victor slides the last tray into the fridge—a process Jamie follows by sound since he isn't quite ready to look directly at Victor— and admits, "Honestly? I have no idea."

The gruff confession startles another laugh out of Jamie, and he looks up despite his best efforts to redirect himself. He finds Victor leaning against the counter with arms crossed, handsome face set into a wry smile.

"There's no shame in an existential crisis," Jamie says.

All the Way Home I'll Be Warm

"I'm not sure it qualifies as a crisis. It's kind of nice, knowing there are no expectations." Victor's smile deepens, his eyes crinkling at the corners. "I mean, it's also terrifying. Never mind finding my own place to live. I need to figure out *who I am* outside of work, and I don't even know where to start. But it's exciting. I could do anything I want."

Jamie bites his lower lip hard. "Anything you want, huh?"

"Anything I want," Victor repeats, grinning.

"As soon as you figure out exactly what that is." Jamie doesn't mean to flirt. He honestly, decisively doesn't. And yet the words slip out with an unmistakably inviting undertone, igniting a sharper glint in the deep brown of Victor's eyes. Suddenly they're both caught in the same desperate pull of gravity, and it takes every scrap of willpower Jamie possesses not to storm across the kitchen and do something disastrous.

They stare at each other for a very long time. And through it all, Jamie's heart races like a wild and treacherous beast.

It's Victor who finally turns away, with a strained laugh and a shake of the head. "One thing at a time," he says.

And Jamie remembers how to breathe.

chapter seven

Christmas Eve dinner is exactly the boisterous and overcrowded affair Jamie has learned to expect from holidays at his parents' house. Family and fictive kin crowd into Warren and Anika's long dining room. The table is designed to comfortably seat twelve people when all the leaves are in place, but it manages, against all logic and reason, to make room for twenty on a mix-and-match assortment of chairs.

Dinner itself—a convoluted potluck of ham, pot roast, turkey, pasta salad, green beans, shepherd's pie, and six kinds of potatoes—is laid out on a long sideboard at one end of the dining room, for want of space on the table itself. Someone even brought one of those terrifying green Jello 'salads', filled with carrot shavings and garnished with mayonnaise.

Jamie loves his extended family, but not quite enough to partake in that particular tradition.

Then again, his plate is full to bursting after only about a third of the food has been passed around the table. Who's even going to notice what he does or doesn't make room for?

The meal itself is an unhurried affair, and Jamie does his best to stay present and attentive. More than once he can feel the overwhelmed edge of all this energy—*too much, too many, too loud*—creeping up on his nerves, but he resists the urge to withdraw.

There are people at this table he hasn't seen since last Christmas, and he refuses to squander an opportunity to catch up with his favorite cousins, his Aunt Bindy, his Great Uncle Seth, his godmother and her wife. So many welcome faces, and yes, Jamie would prefer to interact with them one-on-one, but he hasn't exactly made time for that lately. He hasn't done a great job of staying in touch. And so he's grateful to have this, and he's determined to make the most of it.

All the Way Home I'll Be Warm

The only true downside to the night is that Victor isn't sitting anywhere near him. It's probably for the best. Jamie finds the man distracting enough from clear across the room. He can't imagine how he'd fare if Victor were within reach. But Jamie can't decide if the distance is a matter of random circumstance or if Victor has deliberately put himself as far from Jamie as possible.

By the time dinner is finished, even Jamie's best intentions can't shield him from how exhausted and overstimulated he feels. It's a familiar sensation, especially during a holiday, but also an impetus that Jamie can't continue to override.

"I'll clear the table and pack up the leftovers," he announces, before his mom can throw herself at the task. Aunt Bindy and two of Jamie's cousins offer to help. And though the glance Jamie involuntarily casts down the table makes him confident Victor wants to volunteer too, Warren already has a hand on Victor's shoulder, directing him out of the room with a laugh and a shove.

Everybody else files out too, a single uncoordinated exodus into the living room, where plates of cookies and bowls of candy—including the recently remade buckeyes—have been spread invitingly across the coffee table. Jamie knows the krumkake and cannoli will disappear first, possibly so quickly he won't get to taste either of them this year. But even the rest will be gone by the time everyone departs in the small hours of night.

When the sink is piled high with dirty dishes, and all the voluminous leftovers have been divvied up and packed away, Jamie slips outside instead of following the others to rejoin the party.

He needs to be alone for a while. Just a quick recharge, before he's ready to bury himself back in the messy, affectionate hubbub of his entire extended family.

The front porch crunches beneath his booted feet, ice and new-fallen snow in equal measure. Jamie moves to the far corner—the shadowy edge of the house where no windows can see him—and dusts a bump of snow from the railing so he can lean on the wooden banister. All afternoon, heavy snow fell in big, lazy flakes from a gray sky. Now the freshly dusted layer of it glints in the glow of streetlights and decorations all the way down the avenue. The clouds have since dispersed, leaving the sky above to shine clear as crystal. And even though light pollution sneaks up against the horizon on all sides, the view is still spectacular.

It's a beautiful night, festive and picturesque. It's also *cold*, and Jamie quickly goes from overheated to shivering where he stands. His sweater, thick and soft though it is, can't hope to protect him from the gusty chill.

Jamie straightens up and wraps his arms around himself, wondering if it's worth going back inside for a coat. On the one hand, he's shivering worse by the second, and it won't be long before his teeth start to chatter. On the other hand, if he goes inside, someone's sure to spot him, and his solitude will be forfeit as some well-meaning relative drags him back into the festivities.

His conundrum resolves with the creak and click of the front door behind him—someone's come looking for him after all—and Jamie draws a single, slow breath as he steels himself to turn around. Maybe it will be someone willing to allow him a couple more minutes to himself before dragging him inside for carols or card games or some other form of chaos.

But it's Victor approaching him, footsteps cautious on the slick porch.

And he's carrying Jamie's coat over one arm.

"You forgot your jacket." Victor steps close enough to drape the coat over Jamie's shoulders, then joins him at the edge of the porch. He wears his own thick winter coat, though he hasn't bothered to zip it up, and he slips his hands into the pockets with a wry smile to acknowledge the cold.

"Can't believe you brought my jacket but didn't steal me a cannoli."

"Oh, there's a cannoli in the fridge for you. It's hidden behind the orange juice."

Jamie stares hard at Victor, unable to tell if he's being teased. "You didn't."

"I did. Anika mentioned they're your favorite." Victor meets his stunned expression with a look of mingled apology and curiosity. "Should I not have?"

"Fucking hell, how are you real?" Jamie slips his arms properly into the sleeves of his jacket, then leans once more on the snow-damp banister, making a show of looking out across the brightly decorated neighborhood. He can't look at Victor right now. His heart is already too much of a pulp, over a coat and a stupid dessert. How is he supposed to cope with all that *and* Victor Leone's earnestly handsome face?

Victor hovers uncertainly for only a moment, before sweeping aside enough snow to mimic Jamie's posture. They stand there in silence for something between a minute and an eternity, amiable and yet caught up in a tension that neither of them dares acknowledge aloud.

"You okay?" Victor finally asks, the low rumble of the question breaking through the silence.

"Yeah. I'm good. I just get a little overwhelmed. It's… a lot going on in there." Jamie admits all this with a careless shrug, trusting Victor to understand. The quiet hum Victor breathes in answer feels like a shared conspiracy, and Jamie finally risks looking at him to ask, "You having fun tonight?"

"Sure," Victor says. Jamie raises his eyebrows at the diffidence in that one word, and Victor huffs a sheepish laugh. "I *am* having fun. I promise. But I'm not used to being around this many people."

"Not many big parties in Antarctica?"

"Not much of a social life period. Just my colleagues, my research, and way too much time in the on-site gym."

Jamie figured a rigorous fitness routine must factor into Victor's life, considering the man's muscular frame. He's pretty sure he's heard Victor doing pushups or sit-ups or something through the wall in just the short time they've both been here, which is absolutely not imagery he needs to be pondering.

He sounds only a little breathless when he says, "If I ask what kind of research, will you tell me?" It's a clumsy redirect, but he'll take what he can get.

"I could, but it involves a lot of indecipherable acronyms and jargon about ice cores."

"So it's not top secret government stuff?" Jamie nudges, teasing.

"Not top secret. Just intolerably dull." Victor says this with a smile, looking distinctly amused and… What? Charmed? Fond? Pleased? His eyes have crinkled at the corners, and he's watching Jamie with an intensity to match the pulse in Jamie's own chest.

All the Way Home I'll Be Warm

Suddenly the cold doesn't matter. Jamie's whole body feels warm as he meets Victor's smile with one of his own.

This time, the quiet that follows feels dangerous, or at the very least sharp-edged with potential. Jamie's heart gallops in his chest, and he feels impossibly bold as he leans in and bumps his shoulder against Victor's. Stays there. Waits through the twist of butterflies in his stomach, then thrills when Victor leans harder against him.

There is understanding in this wordless exchange. *Something* is happening here, and Jamie's insides feel feverish with it.

But when Jamie moves to lean even closer—cautious in his approach but unmistakable in his intent—his companion steps abruptly back from the railing.

Victor is still smiling, but there's something pained in the expression now. "I should get back inside," he says, and every word drips with apology and regret and strained self-control.

Jamie hurts, watching him go, and yet he allows it in silence. The door thuds heavily shut, and he stands on the icy, empty porch. Colder than ever now. Alone with his irrational disappointment and his racing heart.

It's not until hours later, back inside, that his mom corners him.

"You've been so quiet since dinner, love," Anika says. "Is everything okay?"

Jamie swallows hard, past a lump of achy emotion and a sudden desire to tell her the truth. There's no way a confession would be anything short of disastrous, unless he somehow extorted a promise from her to not tell Warren. And Anika Phipps is not one for secrets. Neither is Jamie's dad, for that matter. The two have always shared a wide-open honesty that Jamie admires and can't entirely comprehend. Surely no one in his life needs to know every single thought that enters his brain.

But the fact remains: if he tells his mom the truth, he is effectively telling his dad too. And Jamie refuses to throw that kind of wrench into a perfectly pleasant night.

"I'm fine," he says, and it's about two-thirds true. "I've got a lot on my mind, but none of it's bad."

No matter how much it hurts being near Victor Leone without being able to *have him*,

All the Way Home I'll Be Warm

Jamie much prefers this to not knowing Victor at all. If he had a time machine at his fingertips, he wouldn't change a thing about how they met.

"You sure?" Anika peers into his eyes as though trying to suss out all of Jamie's secrets.

"Yeah, Mom." He makes himself smile wryly. "I'm good. I promise." Then he hugs her, quick and fierce, and ensconces himself in the noisiest corner of the living room to avoid further interrogation.

Jamie will get over his heartbreak— hopefully by convincing himself one hookup isn't enough of a connection to be heartbroken over. And maybe, with enough time to repeat the lie, he can make himself believe it.

chapter eight

Christmas morning is, for better *and* worse,
a smaller affair. Lou and Claudia, May and
Jamie, Warren and Anika.

And of course, Victor.

Jamie would rather still be sleeping,
honestly. It's far too early to be awake after
staying up so late for last night's festivities. But
May knocked on his door with too much
enthusiasm to be denied, and Jamie's never been
able to refuse his niece anything.

God, he wishes he could lie to himself well
enough to pretend he'll be able to take a nap
later. He's so exhausted his entire body aches,
after a late night and unsatisfactory sleep.

His mom takes one look at him and fixes
him a mug of coffee—with cream and a little
too much sugar—instead of the hot cider

steaming deliciously in the slow cooker on the counter. There will be time for apple cider later. After Jamie's woken up enough to read his own name written on some of the wrapping paper beneath the tree.

"Thanks," Jamie rasps, and kisses her cheek. He takes a first, long sip of coffee on his way from the kitchen to the living room. And even though a few seconds is not actually long enough for the caffeine to hit his system, that first taste is enough to galvanize him. He feels more human now, at the very least, though his steps are still clumsy and his eyes are grateful to find the living room lit only by the tree itself, the glow from the fireplace, and a single lamp on its lowest setting.

Jamie must not be the only one struggling this morning.

Victor, damn him, looks well-rested and cheerful where he sits with an entire couch to himself. Jamie desperately wants to sit beside him. The urge to just *do it* is almost overwhelming. But a wiser instinct holds him back, painfully aware that there's a nonzero chance he would forget reasonable boundaries the second he got close, and snuggle right in as

though this is something normal between them.
Which would certainly cross a line and probably
make Victor uncomfortable—but even more
apocalyptically, would give up the entire game
to his dad and sister. Warren and Claudia
already sit with their own steam-wafting mugs,
on the other couch and the floor respectively.
There's no way they would fail to notice such an
obvious display.

"Presents?" May asks, when Jamie sits beside
his dad.

"After *everyone* is here," Claudia chides,
bouncing her daughter in her lap. "You know
the rules, monster."

"But it's *forever.*" May sighs theatrically, and
Victor does a remarkably bad job of suppressing
a snicker behind his mug.

The second Lou and Anika finally join the
sleepy atmosphere of the living room—Lou
folding onto the floor beside her wife and
daughter, Anika setting a tray of enormous
cranberry muffins on the coffee table before
carrying her own muffin to the couch beside
Victor—May scrambles up and begins
ransacking the mountain of presents beneath
the tree.

Sorting them is a process of chaotic proportions, thanks to May's insistence on checking every package herself. She can read her own name, but not everyone else's. So each time she finds a present that isn't destined for her own growing pile, she carries it to Claudia, who tells her who to give it to—and then the entire proceeding halts while May imperiously delivers each gift by hand.

On the plus side, this means that by the time anyone starts opening presents, Jamie's had time to finish his coffee and put the last groggy vestiges of sleep behind him. More awake and alert, it's easier to keep his gaze from drifting constantly to Victor's soft smile. His focus slips now and then, but there's plenty else to pay attention to—between the energetic three-year-old, the mug of cider his mom puts in his hand to replace the empty coffee cup, and the wispy tendrils of Christmas music wafting from hidden speakers—and Jamie makes himself be wholly and attentively *here*.

No amount of disappointment or heartache can diminish the overpowering affection he feels for his family, or the way this moment settles beneath his skin and lights him up from the inside.

"Merry Christmas, kiddo," Warren says, when he catches sight of the sappy smile on Jamie's face.

Jamie grins wider. "Merry Christmas, Dad."

Of course, *opening* the presents takes even longer than dividing them up in the first place. The adults in the room would have been content with simply tearing open their gifts simultaneously—but May, with her dragon's hoard five times the size of anyone else's—insists on taking turns, one by one, until everyone else runs out of presents.

It is, all in all, a joyful but time-consuming ordeal. And when it's finally over and someone suggests a group photo, Jamie jumps right up to volunteer as photographer.

"You sure?" Victor gives him a startled look. "I can take the picture so you can all be in it."

"Don't bother, Vic." Warren waves him off. "Jamie hates having his picture taken. Just get in here, you can be his proxy." It's a testament to Victor's good sense—or maybe just his willingness to listen—that he doesn't keep arguing. And Jamie takes the picture with minimal flourish, with the digital camera Anika insists on using.

After that, with the space beneath the tree empty and nowhere else to be, the morning turns comfortably lethargic. Easy conversations, juggling holiday playlists on different phones, drinking hot apple cider, eating muffins. All within a simple shared quiet, and Jamie finds himself relaxing into it more as an observer than a participant. There's no pressure to join the meandering paths of discussion, and it's such a pleasant floating sensation. Cozy perfection, and Victor is just one piece of it. Distracting, still, yes, always, but Jamie can handle this. He can enjoy a morning of warmth and laughter without falling into the same smitten trap that threatened to erode his good sense last night.

Then May grabs Victor by the hand—or rather, by the three of his fingers she's able to wrap her own chubby little grip around—and tugs with all her might. "Victor, come play," she implores, and it takes no extra effort beyond that. In the span of a heartbeat, he's on the floor beside the tree, helping her unpack and assemble some needlessly complicated new farm toy with a singing tractor.

Victor's smile is pure soft humor—and quick as that, Jamie's a wreck all over again.

God damn it, he can't do this. Victor is *too good*, and Jamie can't just sit here pretending not to notice. He doesn't know how the hell he's supposed to survive the rest of Christmas Day, let alone an entire extra month, living side-by-side with this lovely, impossible man—who still wants him, Jamie's got no space in his heart for doubts on that score—and not *have him*.

"I'll be right back," Jamie announces, abandoning his half-finished cider and tugging the phone from his pocket. He glances at the screen, on which the only notification is an unread text he got last night from a high school acquaintance he hasn't spoken to in months, and says, "I missed a call from Sarita."

He's missed no such call, of course. He and his best friend have never bothered calling each other on holidays. Theirs is a friendship best executed in person, which is how they ended up attending the same college halfway across the continent from their hometown, when Jamie has been mostly content to lose touch with everyone else from his graduating class.

But they also make exceptions to their usual aversion to phone calls, for emergencies or disasters or looming crises.

And *this* is a crisis that more than qualifies.

He suits up and takes himself outside for a walk, popping in his earbuds as he calls Sarita's number, so that he can keep both hands stuffed deep in his pockets. The thick scarf he's wearing will probably muffle his words somewhat, but he keeps it bundled high around his face anyway. The sun may be shining in warm scatters between patchy cloud cover, but the wind is intense, and the sheer inescapable fact of *winter* lingers uncomfortably close around him.

The line rings several times—long enough that Jamie's already mentally preparing a voicemail that will convince Sarita to call him without alarming her—before she answers with, "Is someone in the hospital?"

Jamie laughs and spares a glance behind him, along the sidewalk to where his parents' house is now a solid six buildings away. "No. Merry Christmas."

All the Way Home I'll Be Warm

"Merry Christmas," she agrees wryly. "What's wrong?"

"Is now actually an okay time to talk?" Sarita's family doesn't take Christmas nearly as seriously as Jamie's, but it's still a whole thing, with her folks and Sarita herself flying to visit her grandparents in Connecticut. "I can call you later if not."

"Now's a great time to talk. You got me out of a whole interrogation about changing majors at the last minute and needing an extra year to complete my degree."

"Ouch." Jamie flinches in sympathy. "Your parents didn't take it well?"

"Oh, my parents took it great. But everyone else has some questions."

"Why should they be allowed questions? They're not the ones paying for it."

"Agreed. But it's not like I can just hide in the attic until it's time for my return flight. Anyway, like I said. Now's a great time to talk. So tell me what's wrong."

Jamie draws a deep breath, slow enough to brace himself, and confesses, "I'm falling in love with my dad's best friend, and I need you to tell me not to be a complete disaster."

"Oh, sweetheart," Sarita says, sounding suddenly older than him and exasperated by his antics, even though Jamie is the older of them by a solid seven months. "What did you do?"

"Nothing, since finding out who he is."

"Jesus, dude. What about before then? And how did you *not know*?"

"Coincidences happen." Jamie glowers at the icy sidewalk beneath his boots. "It's not my fault the universe decided to throw me in the path of an oncoming train wreck."

"I believe you." Sarita sounds completely sincere, and some of the tightness in Jamie's chest loosens at her willing credulity. "So what happened? Spare me the details, but start from the beginning."

So Jamie does. And even though there's not a damn thing she can do to help—other than make sympathetic noises at all the right intervals—he feels better for having unburdened himself.

It's not until the next day, after Claudia and Lou and May have packed their car, said goodbye amid a flurry of hugs, and left for home, that he realizes Sarita never actually told him to stay away from Victor.

chapter nine

Coexisting with Victor in a quieter house is exactly as torturous as Jamie anticipated, especially once Warren's brief holiday vacation ends and he goes back to work. Anika is ostensibly still around, but she's not much of a buffer. She's simply too busy, between her social life and the time she spends buried in her home office, doing work both paid and volunteer for more charities and nonprofits than Jamie can keep straight.

Which means Jamie has only himself and his own messy brain to find some way to hold the line.

The day he wakes up earlier than usual and nearly collides with Victor in the hall would be bad enough on its own merits. But what sends Jamie into a tailspin is the fact that Victor has clearly just finished his morning workout and is heading toward the shower shirtless and practically glowing, his hair tousled and skin burnished with sweat, face flushed with a warmth that's alarmingly similar to his expression post-orgasm.

Jamie's first reaction, after stumbling to a stop, is a strangled sound at the back of his throat. Then, when Victor just freezes and stares at him, he manages in a strained hiss, "*Seriously*, Vic?" He can't stop his gaze from dipping low, taking in the broad, soft contours of Victor's bared torso and the scandalously low drape of sweatpants over stocky hips.

"You're never up this early," Victor protests, somehow managing to sound both guilty and indignant at the same time.

Jamie closes his eyes and drags in a deliberate breath. When he opens them again, Victor is still standing in the hallway in front of him—still shirtless and tempting and beautiful—but Jamie manages to keep his attention on the man's face. "You're right, sorry." Then, making himself take a firm step back, "I'll stay out of your way."

That afternoon, he accepts an invitation to join some local acquaintances for drinks and burgers, because if he doesn't get out of the house for a while, he will absolutely do something foolish. He borrows his mom's car and spends several hours enjoying the company of his old high school crowd: Malia from the thespian troupe; Laurie from orchestra; Andrew from the school paper; Tamika from every AP class Jamie ever took.

There are a couple people he doesn't actually know, but that's okay. He's content to melt into the ebb and flow while pretending to know what's going on. He puts in an effort to interact when topics veer toward movies he's actually seen, teachers from his old high school, local theater productions. The group is noisy and cheerful, taking up multiple tables shoved together at one end of the restaurant, and Jamie barely has to participate to feel like part of the conversation.

Of course, it's a temporary reprieve.

Even though he's careful not to cross paths with Victor in the morning, by the next day Jamie is right back to antsy and ready to crawl out of his own skin. He feels like a pining heroine from a gothic novel, for all the helpless yearning trapped in his chest. Hell, maybe locking himself in a tower would help. Maybe, if there were some sturdy brick walls between Jamie and the man he can't stop thinking about, it wouldn't be so difficult keeping his thoughts, his hands, his heart to himself.

Or maybe the situation would still be hopeless.

Maybe he never stood a chance.

Just after lunch on December thirtieth, Jamie's phone buzzes with a call from the garage in Mayworth. Thank goodness he programmed the number into his contacts list, or he absolutely would not have answered the incoming call.

"This is Jamie Phipps," he says by way of greeting.

"Jamie, hi," comes a gruff voice from the other end of the line. "I've got good news and bad news."

The brusque words give Jamie pause, and he braces himself to learn that the repairs aren't complete, that they're going to cost significantly more than the initial estimate, that an explosion at the shop destroyed his little vehicle completely.

All the Way Home I'll Be Warm

"Is something else wrong with the car?" he asks cautiously.

"Not at all. The replacement part arrived this morning, and we installed it straightaway. Car's ready for you to pick up."

Okay. That was clearly the good news. "What's the bad news?"

"The garage will be closed both New Year's Eve and New Year's Day. If you want your car before January, you'll need to get here by six."

"Oh." That's not nearly as disastrous as Jamie was fearing. "I think I can do that. Thanks for the update."

He asks his mom for a ride, and is honestly surprised when she says no. Apparently there's too much to do for the big New Year's Eve gala she's coordinating—a fact Jamie probably should've anticipated, since it's a board she's been on for at least six years—and she can't spare eight hours to drive to the North Dakota border and back.

So he says, "I'll ask Dad instead."

"Oh, he won't be able to take you." Anika gives him an apologetic look. "His boss is sending him out on an emergency trip to the San Francisco office. Something about a network outage, and an admin on holiday somewhere completely off grid. His flight leaves in two hours."

"Oh." Jamie blinks, considering how awful it is to spring something like that on an employee—even an incredibly highly paid employee—the day before New Year's Eve. "That's..."

"Awful," Anika agrees with a grimace. "He's not pleased to be going, especially without knowing how soon he'll be able to fly back."

"God, no kidding."

"I'm sure Vic would be willing to drive you," she says, pivoting back to the reason Jamie is standing in her study in the first place. "His schedule's wide open."

It's a terrible suggestion, and Jamie has no plausible pretext to shoot it down. Plus, he wants very badly to do it.

"Good idea," he says, decisive and maybe a little too enthusiastic.

Of course Victor agrees, albeit with a brief hesitation and a flash of something that might be alarm in his eyes. They hit the road a little after one o'clock, stubbornly pretending this is a normal road trip full of normal feelings.

All the Way Home I'll Be Warm

Neither one of them acknowledges the tension that has settled more fiercely than ever into the spaces between them.

Jamie takes a deep breath as Victor merges onto the interstate. It's only three-and-a-half hours to Mayworth, alone and in close proximity with this man he can't have. He just needs to keep up a barricade of harmless small talk and not say anything too honest. He can do this. He can survive a single drive without humiliating himself.

He just needs to keep his eyes on the road, his head in the game, and his heart out of the equation.

*

Jamie fails at all these things.

His surreptitious glances grow more frequent as the drive progresses, even once a clear and sunny sky gives way to cloudy dusk and then early nightfall. Victor Leone is distracting in the glow from the dashboard, and in the passing illumination of streetlights whenever they pass a town. Which would be fine, except that Victor keeps catching him staring.

The look in Victor's eyes isn't the slightest bit quelling. It's comprehension, and heat, and undeniable interest.

There's no way for them to get lost in each other's eyes—Victor's gaze always slides quickly back to the road where it belongs—and yet Jamie's skin buzzes with something dangerously like anticipation.

Small talk hasn't done anything to protect them. They can only delve so far into Jamie's studies, or Victor's nebulous plans for the future, or the books they've been reading. Every path leads right back to truths better left unspoken, and every path makes Jamie all the more sure they both want to speak those truths. He's caught in a tailspin of unacceptable longing, and nudging for details of Victor's work in Antarctica—which are every bit as opaque and incomprehensible as promised—feels like a poor consolation prize next to the deeper intimacy he craves.

It doesn't help that Victor is giving off signals that feel like blatant encouragement, or that the silences rising in the rumbling interior of the car—longer and longer every time—carry such a fraught thrum of potential that Jamie fears he's losing his mind.

They reach Mayworth with forty-five minutes to spare.

Jamie's body is on high alert, his senses reeling with greedy awareness as Victor parks in an open space at the edge of the garage's front lot. After a moment's extra hesitation, the car engine clicks off with a turn of the key, and then.

Silence.

Taut and straining and ready to shatter.

Jamie stares straight ahead across a sidewalk lit by both streetlights and holiday decorations. The sky is dark despite the early hour. A little after five, and yet it feels like they've been driving long enough to leave reality itself behind. Gusty wind blows along the street, and the low-hanging branches of a tree scrape quietly across the roof of Victor's car.

It must have snowed here today, because a fresh, glittery dusting covers everything. The boulevard looks like something out of a fairytale, and Jamie's chest is so full of emotion it's a wonder he doesn't explode.

When their stillness shatters, it's as though both Victor and Jamie are goaded into action by a shared spark. Jamie unbuckles his seatbelt and hears an answering click from across the cab. He lets days of longing translate into momentum, and finds Victor turning to meet him.

Neither of them speaks as Victor's hand slides into Jamie's hair. Jamie's fingers curl at Victor's jaw and slip through the rough stubble of his beard, and they meet in the middle of the bench seat in a kiss that should, by all rights, be awkward and clumsy. But Victor's mouth is demanding and sure, his guiding touch incongruously gentle. And the intensity of the kiss is enough to make Jamie's toes curl in his boots, as he melts for Victor's impossible heat.

Maybe it's the fact that they're so far away from anyone who might judge them. Maybe it's being here in particular, in Mayworth, the tiny Minnesota town where they met as strangers and shared an instant and undeniable connection. Maybe it's just the last goddamn straw finally snapping after days beneath relentless strain—the desire between them too much to resist for a single second longer.

All the Way Home I'll Be Warm

They break apart just enough to breathe, to blink at each other, startled and feverish. Then Jamie climbs into Victor's lap and kisses him again, slipping one arm around the man's massive shoulders, sliding nimble fingers through soft hair. Jamie shivers at the drag of steady hands along his back, and oh, he wishes they were somewhere more private. Somewhere he could touch Victor Leone in all the ways he's been telling himself not to think about.

It's Victor who finally ends this second frantic kiss, gently pushing Jamie away without actually dislodging him from his place astride Victor's lap.

A complicated expression has settled across Victor's face, serious and uncertain, and it knocks Jamie out of his libido-fueled haze and back into reality. Guilt flares up in his own chest—for causing that expression, for crossing a line he has been trying so hard not to cross, for going behind his parents' backs about something so important—but it's tangled up with a frustrated longing that he no longer has the strength to fight.

"You okay?" Jamie asks. Not *What's wrong?* That would be a disingenuous question, when he knows damn well why Victor is looking at him like that.

"Yes. But... God, Jamie." Victor swallows hard, studying him with a scrutiny so piercing through the shadows that it's all Jamie can do not to squirm beneath his gaze. "This is still a bad idea. I want to, but I can't. I won't go behind Warren's back."

Jamie cannot fathom what makes him blurt, quick and thoughtless, "What if we tell him?" As soon as the words are out of his mouth, he recognizes an aching and desperate truth in the suggestion. He is terrified at the thought of having an actual conversation about this with his parents, when he knows how furious they will be, but he also craves it with an intensity he doesn't know how to express.

Victor's answering stillness is so complete that Jamie tenses where he sits astride the man's lap.

He tries to keep his mouth shut, to wait and see what Victor will say, but his pulse is hammering in his ears and he rasps, "You don't want to?" Even as he speaks the question, he is rerouting his thoughts, reevaluating his assumptions, trying to look at the situation from a more reasonable standpoint. Never mind the dire consequences for Victor if they come clean and tell Warren and Anika that they're involved: of course Victor won't want to go all-in on a relationship with someone he's known for a grand total of nine days.

Fuck, what was Jamie thinking?

"Hey." Victor's fingers brush his jaw impossibly gently, tipping Jamie's face up to meet his eyes and not letting him hide. The touch interrupts Jamie's unhappy spiral before it can turn truly frantic, and Victor murmurs, "Stop panicking, sweetheart. You just caught me off guard. I didn't think you were that serious about me. I didn't want to assume."

An unwilling laugh chokes out of Jamie's chest at this, at the absurdity of just how much he wishes Victor *would* assume. "Fucking hell, Vic, of course I'm serious about you."

It's true, even if it is terrifying to admit out loud. He was halfway in love with this man when Victor was a complete stranger Jamie had simply fallen into bed with, infatuated and hoping desperately that they could stay in touch somehow. Of course he's head-over-heels now that they actually know each other.

Complicated history or not, he wouldn't be this tangled up inside over a physical attraction.

Casual sex is one thing. Jamie may not have it often, but he enjoys it just fine. This, though? This is an entirely different problem.

There is nothing casual about the things Jamie feels for Victor Leone.

Victor considers him for several silent seconds. The look in his eyes is unguarded. Warm. Fond. No hint of hesitation or fear. His thumb brushes a soothing rhythm along Jamie's cheek, and Jamie shivers as the arm around his waist tucks him reassuringly tighter to Victor's broad chest.

"If we're going to do this, we absolutely need to tell your folks," Victor says. A smile softens his expression, brighter than the quiet and inevitable shadows of trepidation. "It's the only way I *can* do this. We need to be honest about it."

"When?" Jamie feels suddenly breathless, giddy and terrified and exultant.

"Right away," Victor says firmly. "Tonight. It doesn't really give us time to plan a strategy, but I don't think it can wait. Warren will be pissed no matter what, but the sooner I talk to him the better."

"It can't be tonight. He's out of town for work."

"Oh." Victor blinks at him. "Fuck. I forgot about that."

"We could still tell Mom," Jamie says dubiously, "but it might be a bad idea, if we don't want Dad finding out second hand. This... seems like a conversation that should happen in person."

"How long will he be gone?"

"A couple days, probably?" Jamie's shrug is apologetic. "These emergency trips don't usually take long, but there's no way to be sure. Depends how long it takes him to fix whatever's gone wrong."

"Then we tell him as soon as he gets back. We tell both of them together. If you're sure." A ferocious light glints in Victor's eyes. "*Be sure*, Jamie. This won't be easy for them to accept. We're not choosing the straightforward path here. If you need a couple days to think about it—"

"I'm sure," Jamie interrupts, fierce for all that he keeps his voice low. He tips his forehead against Victor's and closes his eyes for a long moment, making himself breathe. Willing himself calm. "I know what I'm doing. I know what I want."

"Me too," Victor says, gruff and sincere.

And when Victor sounds like that, how can Jamie do anything but kiss him again?

"We should stop," Victor says a few minutes later. He sounds ragged and breathless and so inviting that Jamie wants to cry.

"Why?" He eases back, trying very hard not to stare at Victor's mouth in the dim glow of the streetlight.

Victor's eyes crinkle at the corners, making his whole expression sparkle. "Because, you fucking menace, we're parked next to a public street, and if I keep touching you I'm going to take this too far."

Heat twists, hungry and sharp in Jamie's chest, and he says with heart-pounding hope, "You mean we should stop *for now.*"

"Yes. And you should go, before the garage closes."

"What about later?" Jamie presses, unable to walk away without more tangible reassurance. It wouldn't be unreasonable for Victor to refuse to touch him until everything is out in the open, but Jamie doesn't know how he'll cope if he gets back to Saint Paul and finds himself in the same yearning limbo as before.

"*Later,* we will continue this conversation somewhere more private. Tonight. I promise." Victor kisses Jamie again—one more time, quick and hard and dizzyingly deep—and then growls, "Now get the hell out of my car."

chapter ten

The drive back to Saint Paul is a whole new jittery flavor of torture. Jamie can't even call Victor along the way, because Victor's gorgeous old car absolutely does not have wireless capabilities. And okay, Jamie doesn't actually know anyone who's gotten pulled over for holding a cell phone while driving, but the last thing he wants to do is fuck up Victor's night with some Minnesota law that's probably a very good idea. Especially when they have an important discussion to finish once they're both safely home.

He makes it almost a full hour into the drive before finally surrendering to the need for more distraction than music can provide.

"Two phone calls in a week," Sarita says by way of greeting when she answers. There's poorly suppressed laughter in her voice. "You really *are* in a bad way."

"Nope." Jamie can't keep the grin off his face. "I'm good. Terrific, actually."

"Oh my god, Jamie. What did you do?"

And Jamie can't help it—he can't keep the giddiness locked down a single second longer— he laughs. He should be anxious. He's set himself on a course that will be complicated at best, calamitous at worst. He knows full well the position he's putting Victor in. Jamie refuses to feel guilty for it. The man can make his own damn choices, Jamie's not conning him into anything. But still, someone more pragmatic would surely look at these circumstances with a skeptical eye.

Pragmatism has no place in the delight swirling through Jamie's chest.

"I kissed him," he says now, even though the explanation feels wholly inadequate to explain their heated collision. "Or maybe he kissed me. We just... Look, it was a team effort, okay?"

"I'm probably supposed to feign shock or disapproval here."

"Why bother when you're such a terrible liar?"

"Fuck off, I'm a fantastic liar. I just don't bother lying to *you*." Then, more gently, she says, "You sound happy."

Jamie lets this observation sink in for a moment before admitting, more serious than before, "I really like him."

"You said you were falling in love," Sarita reminds him, a cautious nudge calling back their conversation on Christmas day.

"Yeah," Jamie says. "Fuck. Can we talk about something else? I've got three hours of driving left before I actually get to do anything about this."

"Three hours? Why?"

"Because my car was still in Mayworth. And that's where I kissed him. And now he's got at least a half-hour lead on me, because he drives too fast, and I need distracting."

"Ohhhkay, so he drove you to pick up your car. You know, if you explained stuff in chronological order, I could probably make sense of everything without needing to ask fifty follow-up questions."

"Too much effort," Jamie says. "Tell me about your newest family drama."

"What makes you think there's drama?"

"It's your family. Of course there's drama."

"How dare you," Sarita retorts cheerfully, and then launches into exactly the detailed recounting Jamie's hoping for. The telling fills the better part of two hours, and Jamie doesn't even have to nudge her along once she gets started.

"You know I love you, right?" he says when she finally winds down.

"Same, you sap," Sarita says with long-suffering fondness. Then, reluctantly, she adds, "I should probably go. You gonna be okay?"

"Yes," he says. "G'night. Thanks for keeping me company."

"You're welcome. And goodnight. Try not to get disowned."

Jamie snorts indignantly, but Sarita has already ended the call. He glances at the clock on the dashboard as his car starts automatically playing the same song that paused when he initiated the call. His heart is racing now, with how close he is to home.

He's ready to find Victor—maybe sneak into his room—and interrogate him very, *very* thoroughly about where they go from here.

All the Way Home I'll Be Warm

*

It's not quite ten o'clock when Jamie finally parks in front of his parents' house, simultaneously exhausted and energized, restless with the impatience that's been smoldering inside him since Mayworth.

Victor's car must be in the part of the driveway that winds behind the house, assuming he got back before Jamie—a fact confirmed for him when he steps across the threshold and hears Victor's laugh resonating across the ground floor. Jamie kicks his boots off into a corner of the mudroom and closes the front door firmly behind him, then follows the siren song of Victor's voice. Beyond the stairs, along the hall, past the kitchen. All the way to his mom's study, where Victor and Anika sit in a pair of wing-backed armchairs with a chessboard between them.

"Hey, Mom," Jamie says, making himself address Anika first before allowing himself a cautious glance at the man he hasn't been able to stop thinking about, and adding what he hopes is a casual, "Vic."

"Oh good, you made it home in one piece," Anika says, leaning back from her intense perusal of the game board to give Jamie a distracted smile. "How's the car?"

"Sounds and feels completely normal again. Wasn't cheap, but at least it'll get me safely back to Washington." Jamie takes in the game in progress, hoping it's near completion and then devastated to find that only a couple of pawns and one of Anika's bishops have been taken out of play so far. Fuck, what if Victor's an even match for her? What if this game takes all night?

Jamie knows his mom. Anika Phipps does not pause a game of chess for anything short of an emergency, and she brooks no surrender. Never mind that it's a weeknight and she's got a busy morning tomorrow. She'll stay up until this challenge is complete, no matter the cost.

And there's nothing Jamie can do to extricate Victor from the trap.

When he risks another glance at Victor, he finds a wry apology hidden in the man's lovely smile. Victor clearly recognizes the conundrum, and the secret burn of impatience between them will just have to wait.

All the Way Home I'll Be Warm

"Kick his ass, Mom," Jamie says at last, turning for the hall.

"Hey!" Victor protests, but laughter tinges his affront.

Jamie takes the longest, slowest shower he can manage, refusing to feel guilty about being wasteful after seven-plus hours in a car. He stands beneath the spray until the hot water runs out, and then changes into soft sweatpants and a t-shirt before padding barefoot down to the kitchen. Orange juice is no consolation compared to what Jamie actually wants, but at least loitering in the kitchen means being in the right place at the right time, when Victor excuses himself from the chess board long enough to collect a glass of water.

"How's the game going?" Jamie asks the question at normal volume, tone as casual as he can manage. He makes himself keep leaning against the counter by the sink, resisting the urge to crowd in once Victor gets close— resisting the urge to touch.

"It feels like I'm winning, but that doesn't mean much."

"So you're actually *good* at chess," Jamie observes, offering Victor a wry smile. No one holds their own against Anika otherwise. She doesn't toy with her opponents. If Victor is still in the game, then he's not just good. He's got impressive skills.

"I better be good, after twenty years of letting her kick my ass online." He shrugs, looking self-conscious at the praise, and Jamie senses that he is deliberately downplaying his ability. "I've put a lot of work into improving my game."

"Stubborn," Jamie teases, and it's worth it for the impish smile it earns him.

Victor's voice is soft enough to be discreet when he murmurs, "I'm sorry. I swear, I tried not to get tangled up in anything before you got home, but..."

"It's okay." Jamie keeps his own voice equally low and cautious. "I get it." Victor couldn't very well tell Anika to fuck off even if he wanted to, and there's no way he wanted to, sweet and sincere as he is. This isn't just a question of secrecy and discretion. Victor may not be as close with Anika as he is with Warren, but she's still a friend, and she could not possibly have guessed that Jamie had dibs tonight. There's no world in which Victor would have considered blowing her off without an explanation.

And it's not like either Jamie or Victor can risk telling her the truth yet.

Even in this moment of shared vexation, Victor is watching Jamie with fierce heat, and Jamie makes himself put on a reassuring smile.

"Seriously, Vic, it's okay. Take your time, I'll wait up."

Despite the instant and obvious pleasure on Victor's face, he protests, "You don't need to do that. It's been a long day."

Realistically, Jamie should probably accept the out. But he doesn't care how much of a marathon of waiting he's just signed himself up for. He's not going to surrender so easily. Warmth flares in his chest as he studies Victor's face, and he darts a glance to the empty hallway before leaning in for a fleeting kiss.

"I want to." He feels bold and wild and eager when he backs off. "Come to my room when you're done."

Victor smiles at him, and there is only a faint flicker of heavier shadows behind the smile. "I'll be there." Then he's gone, back into the hall and around the corner—back to his game before Anika has a chance to grow suspicious—and Jamie steadily drains the glass of orange juice, before taking himself upstairs.

He probably shouldn't be surprised that his good intentions don't hold. He does his best to stay awake, reading a book that had him riveted before he started his drive from Washington to Minnesota—though it hasn't much held his attention since Mayworth. It doesn't tide him over now either, though maybe he should have made himself read sitting up instead of sprawled across his bed. With the sleepy ebb of inevitability, Jamie drifts away with his cheek creasing the pages and the light of the bedside lamp sneaking gold through his eyelids.

He wakes, slow and groggy, when a shift of weight makes the mattress creak.

He only remembers the book he was reading when someone plucks it gently out from where it's crushed between his cheek and the pillow. Jamie blinks his eyes open to the sight of Victor leaning past him to set the book on the bedside table.

"Hey." Victor offers a downright sappy smile.

All the Way Home I'll Be Warm

Jamie squirms and adjusts so that he's lying on his back, the better to look up and appreciate the handsome lines of Victor's face cast in soft light and shadow. Victor has one palm braced on the mattress as he perches on the edge of Jamie's narrow bed. His relaxed posture and sparkling eyes tell Jamie an entire story about what's going on in Victor's head, and he doesn't think it's unreasonable to hope those feelings match his own.

"I didn't mean to fall asleep," Jamie says, quiet more from the rasp of sleep than for the sake of caution. They've got the entire second floor to themselves, and at this hour Anika will be at the opposite end of the house below. Yes, they should still be careful, but they're safe enough for the moment.

"It's okay." Victor brushes a lock of sleep-smushed hair back from Jamie's forehead, and the simple gesture is intolerably tender. "It's almost two in the morning."

"Jesus," Jamie groans. "How are you still awake?"

Victor's crow's feet deepen, and his mouth twists into a wry smile. "I drank too much coffee on the last leg of the drive. I don't think I could've slept any earlier even if I wanted to."

"And now?" Jamie surrenders to the impulse to reach out, allowing himself the simple satisfaction of wrapping loose fingers around the wrist Victor's got propped on the bedspread. The bare skin beneath his touch makes Jamie shiver, and he fights off the lethargy still holding his limbs. Not very successfully, but still, he fights. He's too tired to crave anything as energetic as sex, but he'll be damned before he misses a single second of whatever the hell this is.

"Now I'm about ready to hibernate for the rest of the winter," Victor admits.

Jamie grins, sleepy and delighted. "Sounds great. Can I share your cave?"

"Sure." Victor's eyes twinkle even brighter, and he shifts closer on the mattress, until his hip is nudging against Jamie's thigh. "And in the spring I'll catch you some salmon."

Jamie snorts and entertains the barely coherent thought, *Oh, he* is *a bear.* It's a silly, giddy detour and it turns his smile soft at the edges. Despite the heaviness of his eyelids, he can't stop looking at Victor.

All the Way Home I'll Be Warm

"Go back to sleep." Victor leans down to nuzzle a kiss to Jamie's temple, then shifts his weight in an obvious prelude to standing back up. "We'll talk tomorrow." He's going to retreat. He's going to walk through that door and go back to his own room, and Jamie's heart gives a defiant stutter of refusal. The thought of any distance at all between them is enough to make his whole body tighten in protest.

He *doesn't want Victor to go.*

Jamie tightens his grip on the wrist he still holds, a pointed intercept that stops the momentum of retreat. He swallows past a lump of feeling that grabs him momentarily by the throat, holding steady as he meets Victor's curious look and raised eyebrow.

"You could sleep in here."

Victor's other eyebrow rises to match the first, sweeping up toward his hairline. "You sure?"

Jamie nods emphatically before he manages to answer. "Please?"

This time when Victor leans down over him, it's to take Jamie's mouth in a long, languorous kiss. For all the heat humming between them—for all the melting instinct that has Jamie opening for a deeper, delving exploration—there's no teasing suggestion of *more* in this kiss. No nudge toward sex, when both of them are so tired. There is only this quiet, wondering intimacy as Jamie closes his eyes and slides both hands into Victor's hair.

Finally Victor pulls away and murmurs, "Just let me lock the door."

Jamie barely tolerates the sparse seconds in which Victor's heat vanishes. The brief absence is torture. Completely unacceptable. And yet Jamie makes himself wait patiently while Victor returns, shedding superfluous layers of clothing along the way.

By the time Victor slips between the sheets, he's wearing only boxers and a thin gray t-shirt.

Jamie breathes a contented sigh, already drifting off again now that the necessary warm weight has returned to his bed. He rolls away onto his side, but tugs Victor with him by the arm, making it clear distance is not what he's trying to achieve with the maneuver. Thank goodness Victor takes the hint. He cozies along Jamie's back, cautiously at first, then more surely when Jamie wriggles contentedly against his chest.

All the Way Home I'll Be Warm

Jamie tries to wrap Victor's arm more tightly around his waist, but instead has to let go when Victor laughs and reaches up to fumble with the lamp. Only once the room is bathed in darkness does Victor wrap Jamie up in his arms.

It should be strange. Jamie isn't accustomed to sharing his bed, especially for sleep. He should be wakeful and on edge at having someone in his space—even someone as welcome and solid as Victor.

But comfort and fatigue mingle through him, and Jamie quickly fades, down and down, into pleasantly incoherent dreams.

chapter eleven

He wakes unreasonably early the next morning, roused before sunrise by the unfamiliar but welcome inferno of a body snugged along his back. He shivers as his senses come alight, skipping past his usual grudging crawl towards consciousness in favor of an alertness so sudden it makes his heart race.

Desire is the primary emotion roaring for attention and yet, when he squirms around in Victor's arms, he can't bring himself to disturb the sweet, exhausted peace softening the man's handsome face. It's almost enough to make Jamie wish he had any hope of falling back asleep. If he retained even the most tenuous vestiges of drowsiness, he would stay right where he is. Content in Victor's loose embrace and in no hurry to start his day if it means getting out of this bed.

But Jamie is wide awake. The simple fact of waking with Victor in his bed is enough to leave him energized, and frankly horny, and if he stays where he is, he will never be able to keep still and allow Victor to sleep. The temptation to kiss him awake will be impossible to resist.

So instead, Jamie carefully slips out from the circle of Victor's arms—a feat that would not go nearly so well if Victor weren't utterly dead to the world—and dresses quickly and quietly to face the morning.

He almost chickens out when he reaches the kitchen and hears Anika bustling about eating breakfast. His pulse is racing, and it takes him an extra moment, around the corner and out of sight, to steady his breathing and remind himself there's *nothing wrong* with wanting Victor Leone. He doesn't like lying to his mom, even by omission, but this is a temporary problem, and he's not going to let himself spiral over it now.

"Good morning, darling," Anika says when he finally rounds the corner, somehow perfectly enunciating the greeting despite having just put a spoonful of cereal in her mouth.

All the Way Home I'll Be Warm

"Morning," Jamie mumbles, going straight for the coffee pot before he even considers food. By the time he's got his perfect proportions of cream and sugar mixed in, his mom has put an empty bowl in front of his place at the table. So Jamie sits down, steals the cereal box and milk from her, and pours himself some breakfast.

The quiet normally wouldn't grate on his nerves. His family is never especially chatty in the mornings, especially before the caffeine has a chance to kick in. But Jamie can't stop thinking about Victor upstairs, asleep in his bed—and suddenly Jamie is overthinking, worrying about what Victor will think, waking up alone after falling asleep with Jamie in his arms.

Nervous as he is about Anika reading this preoccupation in his expression, Jamie drags his brain onto an adjacent track and asks, "So who won?"

"Won what?" she blinks at him over her cereal.

"The chess match last night. You were still playing when I crashed."

"Oh, Vic did." Anika says this with breezy unconcern that isn't *quite* convincing—she's always been unreasonably competitive—but it's near enough for Jamie to be sure she's not holding a grudge even before she continues, "I made the mistake of sending him a bunch of my favorite chess books for Christmas a few years back. And there might have been an actual chess master on base at one point? He's always been cagey about that bit, but he's difficult to beat these days. Your father refuses to play against either one of us anymore."

Jamie nearly snorts coffee up his nose, surprised into a laugh by the wry petulance in his mom's voice. He sounds only a little choked when he says, "Probably shouldn't have sent nerdy chess books to a man *trapped at the South Pole*, then."

"I wasn't anywhere near the South Pole," Victor cuts in, and the sound of his voice draws Jamie's attention with irresistible force. All Jamie's fears—of Victor being disappointed or worried about waking to an empty bed— evaporate at the heart-melting softness of the smile meeting him from across the kitchen. "Antarctica's huge. Plenty of research stations in plenty of places that aren't the pole."

All the Way Home I'll Be Warm

"How should I have guessed that? You could've been studying ice core samples anywhere," Jamie retorts, and it's all he can do to tamp down the wattage of a smile that threatens to give everything away.

God, he wishes he had Victor alone right now. He wants to crowd close, and kiss him, and hold on with all his strength. He wants these things so desperately that it physically hurts to stay in his chair and put another spoonful of cereal in his mouth.

"I set aside a couple tickets to tonight's gala, in case either of you would like to come," Anika announces into the quiet kitchen. Jamie resists the urge to turn and throw a glance over his shoulder, where he can hear Victor rummaging in the fridge, and instead looks directly at his mom with both eyebrows high. A wry and wordless negative, accompanied by a faint twinge of guilt since he knows Warren isn't here to be her date to the event. Anika laughs and shakes her head. "Yes, my dear, I did anticipate that would be your answer. But I'll always make sure you have the option. Who knows, maybe one day you'll yearn to don a tuxedo and attend a fancy party."

And maybe hell will freeze over thick enough for ice fishing, Jamie thinks but diplomatically does not say.

Instead, he swallows his last bite of cereal and says, "Thanks. I appreciate you. But my answer will always be no."

"What about you, Victor?" Anika says lightly.

The toaster springs, and then Victor is sitting at the table directly across from Jamie, with a blueberry bagel on his plate and a container of cream cheese in his other hand. He gives Anika a beatific smile, only slightly tight around the edges, as he spreads the cream cheese. "It's sweet of you, but I don't think I'm up for anything that involves a big crowd."

"I suppose you probably got out of practice, after twenty years without Warren dragging you to this kind of thing."

"That's a powerful understatement." Victor shrugs. "Not many fancy parties on a research base. But if you... need a plus-one?"

Jamie's insides flip unhappily at the thought, both because he doesn't want to spend New Year's Eve alone while Victor attends some swanky party downtown, and because *Jamie* should have been the one to offer. He suddenly feels like an asshole for refusing to attend the party, because there's no way Victor is any more excited at the prospect than he is.

But Anika only laughs, cheerful and incredulous. "Don't be ridiculous, Vic. I'm not going to pressure you into attending on my account. If you'd rather spend a quiet night in, trapped in this house with my antisocial hermit of a son—"

"Hey!" Jamie protests, despite the fact that this is an accurate assessment. How many social events has he opted out of over the years, purely because he prefers to stay at home with his studies or his books?

Anika reaches over to ruffle his hair, and then stands to put her bowl in the sink. "If either of you has a last minute change of heart, let me know. You can certainly share the limo that will be taking me downtown."

"Thanks, Mom." Jamie absolutely *will not* change his mind. And Victor wouldn't in any case, but from the quick smoldering glance they exchange across the table... There's no fucking way. The two of them are going to have the house to themselves once Anika departs for the gala, and that's too good an opportunity to let slip through their fingers.

The hardest part will be keeping busy until then—and Jamie prays he can maintain a reasonable distance without falling completely apart.

*

The day passes in a painful trudge, as Jamie keeps busy by stubbornness alone. There's only so much laundry, tidying, and reading that can actually fill a day so fraught with anticipation, and more than once he finds himself wishing his mom worked a regular nine-to-five.

By the time she finally leaves—well past a dinner that is thankfully a scattered and meandering affair rather than a coordinated meal—Jamie is ready to climb the walls. Victor has long since disappeared upstairs, and though Jamie hasn't heard any sounds of pacing from the floor above, he's certain hiding away was a desperation move. Every time he's met Victor's eyes today, an electric rush of understanding has passed between them. They're both on edge.

All the Way Home I'll Be Warm

And as Jamie finally sees his mom off at the front door, resplendent in a glittery green evening gown, his mind is already racing upstairs to Victor.

He makes himself lock the deadbolt with steady hands, then climb the stairs at a reasonable pace. It's not precisely that he's embarrassed at his eagerness. He's confident Victor wouldn't judge him for thundering upstairs with noisy impatience. Now that they have the house to themselves, there's nothing to stop them.

But Jamie moves deliberately anyway, letting anticipation pulse through him with the quickening of his heartbeat. A heavy wind keens beyond the sturdy walls of the house, but it can't touch the cozy warmth inside.

Jamie breathes in. Reaches Victor's door just beyond his own. Breathes out.

He barely finishes tapping his knuckles against the woodgrain before Victor calls through the door, "Come on in!"

A fresh surge of heat twists in Jamie's belly, and he turns the knob and steps over the threshold, already searching.

He finds Victor sitting up against the walnut headboard of a bed significantly larger and sturdier than Jamie's own. A thick book sits open on his lap, and he wears a spindly pair of reading glasses that make him look so distinguished the sight takes Jamie's breath away all over again. He hasn't seen Victor wearing those glasses before. Then again, he hasn't really seen Victor reading, since the man seems far more prone to socializing when there are people around. He doesn't share Jamie's habit of hunkering down in any available corner to hide in plain sight behind a paperback.

Victor looks lovely and relaxed, sitting there on top of a perfectly made bed in a pair of soft gray sweatpants and a dark t-shirt.

His eyes crinkle at the corners when he catches Jamie gawping. "Hi there."

"Hi," Jamie agrees in a winded voice. He licks his lips as he watches Victor slip a bookmark between the pages and set the book— along with the delicate reading glasses—on the chest of drawers directly beside the bed. It's only once Victor's eyes are on him again, burning with intent, that Jamie realizes he's still standing in the open door to the hall, his hand on the knob and emotion caught in his throat.

But Victor doesn't tease him. Or nudge him to action. He waits for Jamie to make a move, like he's got all the time in the world for... whatever this is.

Jamie swallows hard and closes the door with a firm click, taking the time to set the lock despite the fact that they're completely alone. Maybe it's superstitious of him, but he's watched too many soap operas to wholly trust an empty house. And anyway, it gives him an extra moment to center himself—to internally shout down the pack of rabid wolves urging him to tear across the room and hurl himself at Victor without thought or precision. Jamie wants to do this right.

He finally shakes off the smitten stupor and crosses the room, tellingly quick despite his best efforts to keep a more measured pace.

"Don't know if you noticed," a teasing note disguises the eager tremble in Jamie's voice, "but the coast is clear." He's reached the bed now and drops to his knees on the squashy mattress, softer than his own. It dips with his weight, with his clumsy forward momentum.

Victor grins and reaches for Jamie. "Then get the hell over here." He tugs Jamie toward him like it's the easiest thing in the world, and Jamie thrills at the strength guiding him forward. An ecstatic shiver rolls along the entire length of his spine as he climbs astride Victor's lap.

This is even better than yesterday in Victor's car. There's no steering wheel digging into the small of his back, no roof to bump his head on and prevent him from sitting up straight, no icy windows or drafty wind. There's just Victor, and his big hands framing Jamie's face with impossible tenderness, reeling him in for a first exploring kiss.

Up until the moment he feels Victor's mouth beneath his own, Jamie expects the kiss to be gentle. He's prepared to goad Victor into something messy and demanding and rough, but he anticipates having to work for it, judging by how careful Victor has been with him before. But they must be even more on the same page than Jamie realized, or maybe Victor's self-restraint is simply stretched too thin. Because without so much as a flicker of hesitation, Victor is kissing him with commanding force.

All the Way Home I'll Be Warm

Jamie thrills at the rough slide of fingers into his hair. He allows himself to be maneuvered, tilts his head obligingly to a better angle at Victor's wordless urging. Even better, he opens immediately at the first impatient touch of Victor's tongue at the seam of his lips, wrapping his arms around broad shoulders and pressing his whole body closer with a needy sound.

He's been waiting for hours, and his senses buzz, hot and incredulous, at the fact that he finally gets to claim what he desperately craves.

Somehow, even though Victor is the exact same man he was in Mayworth, kissing him now feels completely different than it did a few days before Christmas. Hell, there's no reason it should feel like that first time. Not when there are so many new and complicated layers to what started as a straightforward flirtation. They're connected in more ways than either of them knew before, an unexpected lifetime neither of them was even aware of. Between this and their days of mutual longing and denial, how could the two experiences ever compare?

But Jamie is still shocked at how intensely the sensations pour through him. There is something infinitely more urgent in the way Victor touches him. Or maybe the urgency is all tangled up inside Jamie himself—in his own hands, as they slide up Victor's chest and along his jaw and around thickly muscled arms—in his belly, where arousal twists tighter with every passing second.

He loved the way Victor touched him when they were still strangers—the ease of sharing pleasure with no strings attached, simply because they had no reason *not* to indulge the attraction between them. But he loves even more the shocky reverence with which Victor holds him. And even though nothing about this is easy now, every instinct in Jamie's body wants more.

He moans around Victor's tongue when clever hands slip beneath his shirt, palms impossibly warm as they slide up Jamie's back and ignite new fever along his skin.

This is where they would need to stop, if their purpose tonight were anything other than getting completely carried away. This is where Victor would push him back far enough to think. Where sense and reason would reluctantly reassert themselves. Where Jamie would have to find a couple of obedient brain cells willing to engage.

Instead, he drags his fingertips through Victor's beard and nips at the man's soft lower lip. Jamie's eyes are closed, his breath a quiet chaos of panting desperation. He nuzzles in close and tries to catch his breath—fails utterly when Victor curls both hands around Jamie's hips and drags him roughly forward. The maneuver puts Jamie directly over the hard heat of Victor's erection, while giving Jamie's own arousal barely any friction at all.

He doesn't mind, though. He rides down hard, shifting his weight and grinding against Victor—opening his eyes just in time to watch Victor's head thump back against the enormous headboard, an expression of ecstasy written like awe across his face—and Jamie grins at the sight. He still can't entirely believe this man is real, and he rolls his hips again, savoring the strangled sound of pleasure that gets caught in Victor's throat.

Victor's hand tangles again in his hair, dragging him into another devastating kiss. Jamie clings in answer, surrendering without hesitation. And when they finally break apart, both breathing hard, Jamie blinks and stares into piercing brown eyes.

"This okay?" Victor's fingers unwind from his hair, and he rests his hand along Jamie's jaw in the ghost of a touch.

"Yeah." Jamie already sounds wrecked, and he rests both palms on Victor's chest to steady himself. "More than okay. Could be even better though."

A twitch at the corner of Victor's mouth signals that he is actively fighting not to smile, and his eyebrows rise high, crinkling his forehead. "Could it?"

Jamie grins, unrepentant. "We could both be more naked."

A laugh breaks past Victor's thin veneer of control, and his teeth flash in a startled smile. "Shameless imp. What the hell am I going to do with you?"

"I have some suggestions about that too." Except any further irreverence Jamie might offer is cut short by a sudden tug at the hem of his shirt, and the squash of fabric pulling up and over his head. He raises his arms, all too ready to cooperate—then enthusiastically returns the favor, delighted to finally toss Victor's t-shirt over the edge of the bed, to get his hands on bare skin and the dusting of silvery hair that covers Victor's chest.

"God, it's not fair," Jamie groans, ducking forward to bury his face beneath Victor's jaw and nuzzle at his throat.

"What's not fair?" Victor's clever hands are at Jamie's fly now, tugging down the zipper without missing a beat.

"That you're so fucking gorgeous, and *right here*, and I've spent days not allowed to touch you." His hands are roaming unapologetically now. Savoring every inch of heat, of vulnerable skin, of softness and strength finally at his fingertips.

"Ah," Victor breathes, and Jamie can't tell if he's voicing a shared understanding—surely Victor has been suffering too—or if he's gasping at the roving exploration of Jamie's hands.

Jamie laughs and kisses him again, and the sensation of Victor smiling, clumsy and real against his mouth, is enough to set off fireworks inside him.

"Bet you still don't have any goddamn condoms," Jamie mutters when he can finally bear to ease back. He tries to sound wry and flippant about it, but there's no concealing the humor of his tone—or the pleading edge running like a countermelody alongside.

"Nope," Victor confirms cheerfully.

"Maybe we could... I still want to..." Well. So much for wry and flippant. Suddenly Jamie is tripping over his own tongue.

Victor's eyes narrow eloquently. "You'll have to speak more plainly than that."

Jamie swallows back his instinctive shyness at the notion of saying such blunt things aloud. "I'd like to... taste you... this time." Then, before Victor has a chance to catch up or answer, he presses, "Not to make assumptions, but I'm guessing you didn't do a whole lot of hooking up with your colleagues in Antarctica."

This observation earns him a rueful smile and an exasperated shake of Victor's head. "You're right. I did not 'hook up' with *any* of my colleagues. It's... been a long time, honestly."

"Other than me, you mean," Jamie pronounces smugly.

"I do mean," Victor agrees, and it's impossible to miss the way his expression softens with amused affection. "You sure? That's what you want tonight?"

All the Way Home I'll Be Warm

"I really do," Jamie breathes. "I mean... If you're comfortable with..."

"I am." Victor brushes unruly bangs back from Jamie's face. "I trust you. And if I'm entirely honest, I've spent far too many hours already, thinking about your mouth."

"Yeah?" Jamie feels dizzy and pleased, and his mouth twitches with satisfaction even though he hasn't done anything yet.

"You have a beautiful mouth. And I've jerked off more than once, imagining how I might put it to good use."

"Fucking hell, Vic," Jamie groans, dropping his forehead to Victor's shoulder with a helpless shudder. "You can't just say stuff like that when I'm trying not to be a needy disaster."

"Do you want me to apologize?" Victor's smile is audible in every syllable of the question.

"Would you mean it?"

"Lord no." Victor's laugh is dazzling. It fills Jamie's chest and makes his stomach flip, a longing that has quickly become familiar, and thank god he can finally do something about it.

He steels himself against the almost violent blush already creeping up his throat and cheeks, and makes himself meet Victor's lovely eyes—

makes himself ask, aloud and clear, "So you want me to suck your cock?"

Victor's eyes flutter shut and his head thumps back again, his throat working in a visible swallow. Jamie can't take his eyes off him. The man's got no business being so overwhelmingly pretty when Jamie's trying to tease him. It's almost as unfair as telling Jamie he's got a beautiful mouth.

"Yes," Victor rasps. And when he opens his eyes, he stares at the ceiling for an extra heartbeat, as though unsure how else to collect himself. "I want you to suck my cock."

It's by no means a graceful endeavor. There is shared clumsiness in the way they both scramble to finish getting naked, and then Jamie finds other ways to be clumsy all on his own, as Victor settles against the headboard and makes space for Jamie to kneel between his legs.

Maybe this would be easier from the floor. Certainly the angle would be less of a challenge—Jamie's given only a few blow jobs in his life, and all of them involved kneeling on the floor for a partner who was either sitting or standing before him. But Jamie wants to do it like this. He wants to be right here, crowded into Victor's space. Leaning down to take Victor's straining arousal in hand, to tighten his grip and give an exploratory stroke, to duck low and press a teasing string of kisses along the shaft.

He's rewarded for these efforts by a shaky moan and the sight of Victor's hands clenching in the rumpled bedspread.

Without retreating, Jamie tosses Victor an impish smile, then parts his lips and takes the man's waiting cock into his mouth.

This, too, is clumsy and imprecise, but Jamie doesn't waste time being self-conscious about his relative inexperience. He focuses entirely on Victor as he works the rigid length with mouth and hands. He gauges his success by the shallow quickness of Victor's breath, and takes as much as he can without choking. He savors each grunt and moan and gasp, as he strokes his fist in imperfect rhythm with the efforts of his lips and tongue.

He pulls off completely now and then, to nuzzle in alongside and trace ghosting kisses along silky flesh.

All the while he marvels at Victor's self-restraint, until at last he can't stand the way

Victor is clinging to the comforter instead of him—and reaches out to guide one of those strong, sturdy hands to the back of his head.

Victor's answering groan is a low rumble, rough as sandpaper and deep as the sea. But he takes the hint. He tangles his fingers in the wild strands of Jamie's hair and—though he's obviously careful not to be too pushy—holds on with a frantic intensity just shy of wresting away Jamie's control.

It's a knife's edge of satisfaction, and Jamie thrills at the sensation of it. The intimacy of this gorgeous man, on the cusp of losing control and yet trying so hard to be careful of him. Even in this new, needy roughness, there is reverence in the strength of Victor's touch. Jamie works his cock more feverishly than ever, caught between the need to make this last and the desire to see Victor come.

"*Jamie*," Victor gasps, more pointed than a simple expression of pleasure.

Victor's been growling and muttering all kinds of things, praise and affection and hungry fragments. But this is different, and Jamie takes it for the warning it is, retreating just in time for Victor's orgasm to catch him across the throat and chin. He raises his eyes to take in the overwhelmed bliss written across Victor's handsome and expressive face.

"Jesus, Jamie." Victor sounds wrecked, as he unwinds his grip from Jamie's hair and slumps against the headboard in a pose of lethargic satisfaction.

Jamie can feel his own eyes sparkling with mischief—and with unsated desire of his own—as he wipes the back of his hand across his face, probably doing a terrible job of making himself presentable.

Victor drags him in for an unsteady kiss, deep and fast and plundering.

Then, before Jamie can gather enough breath to ask, *What now*, he finds himself shoved onto his back, Victor's powerful hands pushing him down along the mattress and guiding his thighs apart with impatient strength.

Jamie is so caught up in this manhandling—and in his own enjoyment of just how easily Victor pushes him around—that he startles when Victor goes still above him. The last thing he expects is hesitation. And when he blinks lust-bleary eyes and actually makes himself focus, he realizes hesitation is not at all what this is. Caution, yes, but completely deliberate. Victor has moved into the space between Jamie's knees and is watching him, patient and steady. Waiting for confirmation that Jamie is actually with him before continuing.

"My turn?" Victor asks, and the gravel of his voice sends a shiver the entire length of Jamie's spine.

"God yes." There is not enough *yes* in the world to express what Jamie is feeling in this moment, and he spreads his legs wider. Inhales sharply when Victor leans down, hot breath sending shivers along Jamie's overheated skin.

Victor touches him, light and unhurried. Guides Jamie's legs up over Victor's shoulders. He nuzzles at Jamie's thigh, his stomach, the hollow of his hip.

Then he puts his mouth where Jamie actually needs it, and everything else—every irrelevant piece of reality outside this house, this room, this bed—disappears.

chapter twelve

It's too early to sleep. In the soft and satisfied moments after orgasm, Jamie and Victor get dressed—both of them in the clothes they were already wearing, though Victor also takes the time to tug a sweater over his head—and make themselves comfortable on one of the couches downstairs. Only after checking to make sure they really do still have sole run of the house does Jamie let himself snuggle into Victor's side. The arm that drapes across his shoulders, tucking him close, warms him more than any throw blanket ever could, and Jamie exhales, slow and content.

He hears Victor breathe a matching, barely audible sigh, as Jamie snuggles in tighter along his side and wraps a loose arm around his waist, relaxing against his chest.

The Phipps residence has normal cable, so they flip through channels until settling on a Star Trek marathon that suits them both. Neither of them is paying much attention to the episode. Jamie's not, at any rate. And some subtle tell makes him just as certain he has Victor's full focus.

It's not tension, exactly. But despite the easy way they've wrapped themselves up in each other, some lingering energy hovers unanswered between them. Waiting to be acknowledged.

Jamie feels ridiculous for needing the reassurance, but he murmurs, "You okay?"

"I will be." Victor presses a kiss to the crown of his head.

Jamie shivers at the sweet sensation, but presses stubbornly on. "You feel guilty." He doesn't mean to sound petulant. Of course Victor's going to have complicated feelings about everything they just did. Hasn't Jamie been tangled up over this for days? Just because he's decided having Victor is worth the complications, doesn't mean Victor can just decide to be at ease with crossing so many lines with him.

All the Way Home I'll Be Warm

But Victor's rumbling laughter—so quiet Jamie doesn't so much hear it, as feel it where his head is tucked to Victor's chest—makes his sincerity obvious when he answers, "Not guilty enough to regret anything."

"Good," Jamie says, and adjusts his position just long enough to press a quick kiss to Victor's cheek before burrowing back in.

It's not even ten o'clock yet, and Jamie lets himself melt with the prospect of being able to spend tonight just like this. His parents never get back from these types of galas before two in the morning, and even if Anika comes home earlier than usual on account of attending alone, the living room is close enough to the front of the house that he'll hear the limo pull up. He spent his childhood taking opportunities exactly like this one to watch all sorts of movies and television he wasn't supposed to see, and he knows exactly what to listen for.

The commercial breaks and spaces between episodes are full of a sporadic countdown to midnight, which Jamie cares about even less than the long-ago-memorized episodes of a beloved show.

Despite the lazy contentment rolling
through him like a current, it doesn't take long
for Jamie to get caught up in his own head. He
tries to keep his mouth shut. To just let himself
enjoy this, and not get stuck on Victor's words.

I will be.

Which means he's not okay now.

"Is this too weird?" Jamie asks, when he can
no longer hold the anxiety unspoken in his
chest.

He's not especially heartened by the long
silence that precedes the answer, but he trusts
the earnest calm when Victor's voice finally
comes. "No. I mean yes, it's weird, I can't deny
that. But it's not..." A pause. A longer
consideration, a weighing of words so careful
that Jamie can tell that's exactly what's
happening, even before Victor continues more
softly, "I'm not sure I can describe the cognitive
dissonance I'm feeling right now. Knowing you,
like this, but also as Warren's son... It's abstract,
but it's there. This memory of all the years
Warren spent talking about you, all the stories
he told me about his kids, how proud he's always
been of you and Claudia."

"He talks about you all the time too," Jamie admits. "But it was hard to think of you as a person when I never really saw any pictures, or met you, or even talked to you."

"Yeah." Victor chuckles wryly. He gives a shrug that jostles Jamie, then adds with a stubborn air, "I'll square it all up in my head eventually."

They lapse quiet together again, and drift in their lovely liminal space for so long that Jamie startles when Victor says, "I should've recognized you in that bar." There's an almost grumpy growl undercutting the words—a grousing sheepishness that has no business making Jamie smile—but it does, especially when Victor's arm squeezes around him. Holding him tighter than ever, as though he doesn't want his words to be mistaken for discouragement. "Warren sent so many pictures of you over the years, before you got all camera shy."

Jamie *hmms* a sound too neutral to count as agreement. He doesn't blame Victor for not recognizing him, in a strange town with no connection to either of them, based solely on knowledge gleaned from photos taken before Jamie started junior high.

"I'm glad you didn't recognize me," Jamie admits, low and confessional. "If I'd known who you were, I honestly don't know what... It would've been *different.* We never could have done this. But I think I still would have wanted to."

"Or you would've immediately relegated me to the Friend Zone, which is where I belong," Victor teases. But there's a faint bite of self-deprecation in the words, and it's enough to tell Jamie that Victor wouldn't have noticed him— not like this—if they'd met with their eyes open. Whatever alchemy of oblivious opportunity protected them in Mayworth, it's the only reason Victor is able to see him as a sexual partner.

Maybe that should bother Jamie more. Maybe he should be more mindful of the strange and uncomfortable position their relationship—nebulous and nascent as it is— puts Victor in.

Or maybe he should relax and enjoy this closeness, and leave the overthinking for later, when his dad comes home and it's time for difficult conversations. It will be a new year, after all. It's as close as they're going to get to a blank slate.

Midnight sneaks up on them by unhurried degrees, and Jamie would probably have missed the moment entirely if not for an interlude between episodes doing a final countdown to the new year. Footage of the ball dropping in New York City, though the event must've been recorded an hour ago. Jamie moves despite the sleepiness in his limbs—sets his hand to Victor's chest—pushes himself up to make a wordless and irrefutable demand for a kiss. It's tradition, after all. And Jamie's never had someone to kiss at midnight before.

Victor smiles into the press of Jamie's lips, then curls a hand at Jamie's nape a moment later as though to signal he's taking the kiss more seriously.

They linger in it, indulging themselves, exploring all over again. *Contentment* isn't a strong enough word to describe what Jamie is feeling in this moment, as he gives himself over without regret. Victor tastes like the cinnamon cider they've both been drinking, his mouth soft and patient beneath Jamie's, his hands both tender and restless as they touch him. It's enough to make Jamie feel lightheaded and warm and unapologetically sappy.

There's still so much they haven't negotiated, when it comes to the contours of their relationship and what they're actually going to tell his parents, but those uncertainties can't touch him when Victor is kissing him like this.

Every kiss has to end eventually, and when Jamie subsides and melts along Victor's side once more, it doesn't take long for reality to creep in around him with its unanswered questions. He does his best to ignore everything but the steady rise and fall of Victor's chest beneath his palm, the comforting warmth between them, the familiar music from the television as the opening credits signal another episode beginning.

"What's wrong, sweetheart?" Victor asks, and Jamie huffs a wry laugh.

"Nothing's wrong," he answers truthfully. The fact that he's a little terrified to face the consequences doesn't mean he doubts his decision. He's never felt like this with a partner before—this blissful or open—this settled in his own skin, even as the world crowds close with outward complications. He feels so naturally at ease with Victor, and has since the moment they met. Maybe that's why he couldn't bear to simply let go.

"Then what are you thinking about?" Victor presses.

"Just getting stuck in my own head," Jamie admits. "We should probably come up with a strategy. Figure out how to tell my parents, and not just wing it when we finally get them both in one place."

"You think strategy will help?" Victor's tone is deliberately light, and he nudges a kiss to Jamie's cheek as though to soften the question. "They're not going to take it well regardless."

"I know." Jamie sighs and nuzzles into the collar of Victor's sweater. "And it'll be way worse for you than me. They've always been overprotective."

This fact is high on the list of reasons Jamie went to college thirteen-hundred miles away. By the time he graduated high school, he needed distance more than anything else—a chance to prove he wasn't a helpless child, and to figure out who he was outside the cloying weight of his parents' vigilance. Now he's nearly within reach of his degree, starting grad school in the fall, and his parents are better about remembering he's a goddamn adult, but still not great.

They're going to take one look at Jamie falling for Victor and assume he doesn't know what he's doing.

"They want what's best for you." Victor kisses the crown of his head and wraps both arms tighter around him.

"I'm twenty-two years old. They aren't the resident experts on what's best for me anymore."

"Even so," Victor murmurs. "We'll have our work cut out for us, convincing them *I'm* good for you."

Jamie squirms upright again, bracing a palm on Victor's chest—directly over his heart—as he peers into Victor's face. "*You* believe it though. Don't you?"

Victor's smile is small, but it crinkles the corners of his eyes. "Damn right I do. I wouldn't be here otherwise." *Like this*, he obviously means. With Jamie on this couch. Tangled up and disoriented, diving headfirst into a serious relationship with a man half his age.

"Good." Jamie gives a decisive nod. "Now. How the hell do we convince my parents to hear us out before they lose their shit."

"Step one: we'll probably need to convince them we didn't spend Christmas sneaking around behind their backs." Victor says this with an imperfect effort at levity, a more honest strain of worry glinting through the facade. "Which might be tricky, considering we're technically sneaking around behind their backs *now.*"

"Leave that part to me." Jamie cracks what he hopes is a reassuring smile. "I've always been a terrible liar. They'll have to believe me when I don't crumble under their combined interrogations."

"Fantastic," Victor deadpans. "In that case, step two: avoid letting either of your parents punch me in the dick."

Jamie snorts. "Oh, that part's easy. You should be safe if you stand behind me."

"Good. Then step three: find exactly the right words to convince them I'm not fucking around or taking advantage of you." Which is where the real challenge will lie, and they both know it. Jamie knows with his entire soul that

Victor would never do anything to hurt him, that his own heart is right about this man, that he and Victor could be good together if they stay on this path. And he hopes like hell that Warren trusts Victor enough to move past the inevitable sense of betrayal and remember that Victor is a good man.

"We'll convince them," Jamie says, pulse fluttering at the earnest edge of his own voice. "I'm not sure how yet, but we will. We'll make them see that this is real."

He wonders, with an undeniable pulse of guilt, if Warren will be able to forgive Victor. Jamie fears his parents' anger—he so rarely needs to face it head-on—but at the end of the day they'll still be his parents, no matter how well or badly this conversation goes. But Victor is risking his closest friendship to be with Jamie, and there's no way Warren will be anything short of furious when he first learns the truth. What if he can't move past that? What if Jamie can't convince him? What if the two men can't be friends anymore, even once Warren believes this relationship is something Jamie truly wants?

All the Way Home I'll Be Warm

He resists the urge to ask these questions aloud. There's no way Victor hasn't considered them, and if he's decided Jamie is worth the risk—is worth the potential consequences—it sure as hell isn't Jamie's place to try and talk him out of it.

"It's late," Victor says, and the words belatedly knock Jamie out of his spiraling thoughts. "We should probably get some sleep."

Before Anika gets home, Jamie silently agrees. "Together?" he asks hopefully.

Victor's eyes crinkle at the corners. "Sure." And then, with a soft look. "Happy New Year, sweetheart."

chapter thirteen

Jamie would just as soon sleep in until noon the next day—what better way to celebrate the new year—but even their late night isn't enough to dissuade Victor from his habitual morning routine. Still, Jamie makes a decisive attempt to keep Victor in bed. He's downright shameless, kissing him soundly and being an absolute flirt about the whole thing, but Victor is too stubborn. Soon enough, despite Jamie's best efforts to distract him, Victor slips out of bed with a smile and a wink, leaving Jamie too wide awake to doze any later into the morning.

He makes his way downstairs still in pajamas, and startles when he finds his mom already in the kitchen, drinking coffee. She looks completely put together and ready to start her day, which honestly isn't fair considering she had an even later night than Jamie.

She seems equally surprised to see him, despite the fact that he's clearly rolled right out of bed and come in search of breakfast. The fact that he can't stop smiling is probably throwing her off even more than his presence. Being up at this hour voluntarily isn't completely unprecedented, but his early-morning cheerfulness certainly is.

"Happy New Year, love." She takes a last long sip of coffee and then rises from her chair, the movement quick and graceful as she puts her mug in the sink.

"Happy New Year," he agrees, still grinning like a sap as he lets himself be swept into a tight hug. "How was the party?"

"An unsurpassed masterpiece," Anika declares, letting him go with an indulgent ruffle of his already sleep-tousled hair. "Never before has so extravagant a gala been so flawlessly achieved."

"I meant did you have fun?" Jamie barely stifles a laugh at his mom's unconcealed delight. She has every right to be pleased that the event she's been so meticulously planning went off without a hitch—but that doesn't mean he's not allowed to tease her.

"Of course, darling." She kisses him on the cheek. "Success is always fun."

Then, feeling not at all sneaky about it, Jamie asks, "Have you heard from Dad yet today?"

"Oh, yes." Anika beams. "He's traveling. Home today for sure. Now, if you'll forgive me, I need to be off before I'm late."

"Late for what?" Jamie blinks at her, not bothering to conceal his perplexity. "It's New Year's Day."

"Brunch," she says, which sounds ludicrous to Jamie considering the early hour, but then he's never understood the ways of people who actually like mornings. "I'll be home for supper, though."

Then, with a second quick hug, she's out the kitchen door and vanishing down the hall. Jamie listens for the clipped steps of the high-heeled shoes she slips into, and then the heavy thud of the front door as it swings shut behind her.

Only after she's gone does it occur to him that he probably should've asked *when* today. He can't extrapolate the ETA of a flight from San Francisco if he doesn't know when his dad boarded the plane. How is he supposed to guess whether he and Victor have a few hours or all damn day to talk through contingencies, if he doesn't know when Warren's flight is supposed to arrive?

"Huh," Jamie says. And then, maybe because the empty kitchen is a little disconcerting, or maybe because the silence feels wrong somehow in the face of his own buoyant mood, he turns on the little radio that lives on the windowsill above the sink. It takes only a moment to scan the channels until he finds the upbeat opening notes of some classic rock anthem he halfway recognizes.

He's cleaning up his own empty breakfast dishes when Victor joins him, and Jamie makes no effort to conceal how much he appreciates the tight gray t-shirt and well-worn blue jeans Victor has chosen for the day. He grabs a mug from the cupboard before Victor has even finished crossing the kitchen, pouring the last of the coffee into it and holding it out like an offering. Victor quirks an eyebrow and a glance, first at the coffee, then at the radio still playing a little bit too loud in the corner, then at Jamie's blatantly teasing smile.

All the Way Home I'll Be Warm

"You're in a good mood," Victor observes, mouth twitching at one corner.

"Obviously." Jamie gestures with the mug. "Do you want coffee or not? You don't even need to fight Mom for it, she's gone out for the day."

Comprehension smoothes Victor's expression, alongside a soft hint of amusement. "That so?" And then he's crossing the wide kitchen, moving right past the table to close in on Jamie and take the mug from his hand. When he leans down and kisses Jamie's cheek, Jamie follows instead of letting him draw back too quickly, tangling a hand in Victor's hair and tugging him into a longer kiss.

Victor laughs when Jamie finally lets him go, the sound a delighted rumble. "You're still a complete menace."

"Rude," Jamie says cheerfully. "Not even a thank you for the coffee."

"Thank you for the coffee," Victor tries to deadpan, but the glint of humor shines through anyway.

"I'm going to get dressed." Jamie makes himself step back and away. He barely resists the temptation to steal the mug right back out of Victor's hands, to set it aside on the nearest counter so that Jamie can thoroughly debauch him instead. They can afford a little patience. They have the morning to themselves, and the novelty of this fact makes Jamie feel bright and buzzy inside. He doesn't even mind Victor's obvious amusement at his expense, wrapped up as it is in fondness and anticipation.

He finds himself caught in a spiral of more anxious thoughts once he's alone, as he hurries upstairs and digs through the dresser drawers. His mind keeps playing over last night's conversation, and the inescapable fact that he has no idea how best to approach his parents about Victor.

There's a chance they'll take the revelation in stride—that they'll trust Jamie to know what he's talking about—but it's a slim chance. Even if he could delude himself into hoping this were a likely outcome on its merits, Victor isn't just any older man Jamie's taken up with. He's *Victor*. Warren and Anika will be discomfited and disappointed at best, furious and wounded at worst, with a whole swathe of other tangled reactions in between. And Jamie knows which end of the spectrum is more likely.

All the Way Home I'll Be Warm

No brilliant revelations find him in the moments he spends changing into a pair of badly rumpled jeans and a thick green sweater. But that's all right. They'll have time to brainstorm today. Victor's a clever man. Surely he'll come up with plenty of ideas Jamie hasn't thought of.

At the base of the stairs, Jamie stumbles and nearly trips on the bottom step. A massive black suitcase stands against the wall near the front door, taking up an inordinate portion of the mudroom. He didn't see it there in his rush to get upstairs. But he didn't hear the front door slam while he was changing, either. How long has his dad been home?

An unpleasant tightness twists in Jamie's chest, catching his voice and stopping him from calling across the house. Nerves, trepidation, uncertainty. A heavy pulse of anticipation thrums behind his ribs, fearful and unwelcome, and now he's hurrying for different reasons than before. His bare feet make almost no sound on the wood floor as he rushes back toward the kitchen—toward Victor—and then stops just short of rounding the corner when he catches

Warren's voice rising like a thunderclap through the quiet house.

"—*the fuck* you think you're doing with my son?"

"Warren—" Victor's voice comes firm and strong, but whatever reply he intends to make, Warren doesn't let him speak.

"Don't. You don't get to play it like I'm the asshole here." Wrath turns the interruption ragged and sharp beneath tenuous control. "Something was weird with you two from the goddamn start. I told myself I was just being paranoid. Reading too much into things. Surely my *best friend* wouldn't betray my trust."

Jamie's heart clatters in his chest. There's no space to wonder if Warren saw them. Of course he did. From the hall? Through the kitchen window? It hardly matters which. And Jamie knows, he knows, *he knows* he needs to announce his presence. Join Victor and his dad in the kitchen, try to get control of this awful confrontation. Do his best to mitigate the damage.

So much for coming up with a plan. This wasn't how Warren should have found out. They were going to tell him. And risk his anger, yes, but not like this. Not like criminals caught with something to hide.

He should step around the corner and put himself at the center of the conversation, but he stays right where he is, breathless and listening and pretending to himself that he's waiting for the right moment to intervene.

It feels like an impossibly long time before Victor finally answers, sounding impressively steady. "Jamie and I have an understanding. We were going to tell you—"

"The hell you were!" Warren snarls.

"You don't have to believe me," Victor says, bland tone belying the tension straining beneath. Jamie can picture vividly the way he probably shrugs with the words, the wry apology written across his handsome face as he stares down Warren's accusations.

"You haven't even been here two weeks," Warren says. "What the fuck did you do?"

The next pause lasts so long that Jamie's terrified stillness nearly shatters—but the instant before Jamie breaks enough to enter the fray, Victor answers in a tone of graveled steel. "You don't get to take that tone with me. You have every right to be angry. I lied to you by omission, if nothing else. But I'm not some predator taking advantage of your son."

"He's just a kid!"

"He's twenty-two and perfectly capable of making his own decisions," Victor counters with forceful calm. "And he'd be pissed if he heard you talking about him like that."

"*You* do not get to lecture *me* about my son," Warren bites out.

"You should talk to him."

"I'm talking to you. You're the goddamn adult here."

Jamie bristles, even as he finds himself completely unsurprised at hearing his dad fall on the stifling fiction that Jamie isn't a grown man capable of managing his own love life.

But Victor is already answering, voice dipping so low it almost fails to carry around the corner. "Jamie isn't a child, Warren."

"You're twice his age. Hell, more than twice his age. How can you expect me to be okay with this?" Warren's voice rises with every word, and by the end he is very nearly shouting.

Victor's answer comes quiet and tight. "We were hoping to make our case and give you time to think it through. I'm sorry it didn't work out that way."

"Fuck you." Warren's words drop so low and icy that Jamie's hands clench into fists at his sides. "How did this even happen? How do you go from hooking up with some hot young twink with car trouble to sleeping with my son less than two weeks later?"

Silence answers this question, strained and awful and almost absurd enough to be funny.

"Oh, fuck no." Warren's voice is shaking now. Connecting these particular dots has clearly catapulted him to new heights of rage.

"Warren—"

"My son is the hot young twink? Are you goddamn kidding me?"

"I didn't realize he was your Jamie."

"How could you *not realize*?"

"It's not like we exchanged personal information. Maybe if you'd named him something like Horatio or Malachi, I would've asked more questions." There's humor in Victor's protest, but it carries an edge so sharp it stings. Defensiveness, anger, hurt, self-deprecation. A complicated and painful muddle that makes Jamie's chest hurt.

"I invited you into my home." Anger seeps into the cracks and crevices of every sandpaper syllable. "I trusted you with my family."

"I haven't done anything to hurt your family. I let *you* down, but that's got nothing to do with Jamie."

"Stay away from him, Vic."

"No." The word is blunt. Simple. Sturdy. So confident and sure that new calm washes over Jamie's frantic senses. God, he can picture this too: Warren glowering and clenching his jaw hard enough to grind teeth; Victor meeting that stare with pained but level confidence.

"I want you out of my house," Warren says. "If you're not gone by the end of the day, I won't be responsible for the consequences."

The threat unlocks Jamie's lost momentum, and he finds himself stumbling forward, shoving himself around the corner and through the doorway into the kitchen. No more cowering at the periphery of a confrontation he should've joined from the start. Enough is enough.

"You can't send Victor away." He takes a quick measure of the room. Victor stands near the table, broad shoulders beset by tension and his countenance grim. Warren has frozen a few steps away and looks ready to tear him to pieces. Jamie strides quickly across the room to put himself directly between the two men. He faces off against Warren and tries to look more steady than he feels. "Are you seriously threatening him, Dad? Have you lost your entire mind? What next? Are you gonna challenge him to a duel in defense of my virtue?"

"Jamie." Warren closes his eyes, rubbing hard at the bridge of his nose. If Jamie weren't so angry, he might be impressed at how quickly his dad has switched from fury to exasperation, as Warren mutters, "Can we not—"

"You started this," Jamie snaps. Protective rage surges and roils inside him like storm clouds.

Warren levels Jamie with a guarded look, straightening his posture deliberately. "It's my house. And I don't want that treacherous piece of shit staying here one more second." He says this without looking at Victor, but the blow lands just the same. Jamie can't see Victor, but he hears the wounded intake of a single sharp breath.

Fury clatters loose in his chest.

"Don't talk about him that way," Jamie says through gritted teeth. He unclenches his jaw with difficulty as he turns to catch Victor's eye. "You don't need to stay for this. But don't you dare pack your bags."

There's a lingering shadow of hurt in Victor's face—how could there not be, after everything Warren just threw at him?—but he gives Jamie a small smile, fond and real. Then he's gone, disappearing around the corner, footsteps fading along the hall. Leaving Jamie alone with his dad, in the bright contours of a kitchen that has never before felt quite this claustrophobic. The warm woodgrain of the cabinets catches sunlight through the big windows, and the stone countertops glitter and shine. It's all such a dramatic contrast to the ugly knot of anger and guilt tangling in Jamie's gut, as he stares his dad down.

He wonders if he's made a strategic error. With Victor at his back, it was easy to stand up to Warren. On his own, the challenge feels nearly insurmountable. Warren Phipps has always been a persuasive force of nature, his disappointment one of the worst punishments Jamie could imagine. Standing alone, Jamie struggles to maintain a confident posture, despite how livid he is. He feels the call of old patterns, the involuntary deference threatening to worm beneath his skin alongside a lifetime of deep respect.

He makes himself square up, a conscious effort that nearly crumbles when—instead of the fresh wave of anger he expects—he's met with Warren collapsing into a chair at the long kitchen table.

Warren doesn't look angry now. He looks devastated, and sad, and the visible change in demeanor makes Jamie's stomach flip.

"Are you okay?" Warren asks, and the question sets off a violent contradiction of reactions in Jamie's chest. He's offended by the implication that Victor would ever do him harm. He's heartbroken at the sincerity of his dad's fear. He's sick with the guilt of having put that shattered look on Warren's face.

"Victor would never hurt me." Jamie speaks quietly, but the words ring firm with certainty.

"You don't know Victor."

"But you do." Jamie takes a cautious step forward. "And I know him better than you think."

Rationally, Jamie can acknowledge that ten days is nowhere near enough time to explain the depth of emotion he feels, or his desperation to know Victor even better, in every possible way. But his heart has never steered him wrong before, and he's not going to start mistrusting it now.

"You met him *once*," Warren protests. "Decades ago. I wasn't sure you even remembered him."

"I didn't," Jamie admits. "But we've been spending time together. I like him a lot, Dad. I like being with him." He doesn't mean the statement to sound sexual, but maybe he should've chosen his words more carefully— because Warren tenses again, fast and sharp, as though Jamie just slapped him across the face.

"He's too old for you," Warren says, and the rough, almost choked-off gravel of his tone makes it clear that this is the least of the protests he wants to lodge.

"Maybe." Jamie claims a chair partway down the table, tucking one foot up onto the seat and wrapping his arms around his folded leg. "Doesn't change how I feel. Or the fact that it's my decision to make."

All the Way Home I'll Be Warm

What Jamie staunchly does not say, despite the strength of the sentiment trying to burst from his chest, is that he's falling in love with Victor Leone. He's falling fast, and hard, and with an intensity he's never experienced before. It's overwhelming, but he doesn't want to stop.

"What am I supposed to do with this?" Warren stares at Jamie with shattered disbelief. "You can't ask me to condone this... this... relationship? Is that what we're talking about here? Or are you two just fooling around?"

Ire rekindles and flares in Jamie's chest, and he puts his foot back on the floor with a jerky movement. He sits straighter, narrows his eyes, and meets Warren with a defiant glare.

"Fuck off, Dad. Even if we are just messing around, what we do together isn't any of your business."

At least Warren has the good grace to look chagrined. "You're right." Then, to Jamie's unvarnished shock, he adds, "That was out of line. I'm sorry."

Jamie considers for a long moment, before finally taking pity and speaking in a tone that is gentler, if not quite conciliatory. "I'm not asking you to be okay with this right away. I'm asking you to think about it. And stop being a dick to Victor. I know we caught you off guard, and it probably looks like we've been sneaking around this whole time. But I swear we haven't. This is new for us too."

A hundred questions burn in Warren's eyes, alongside a hundred other things. Incredulity. Desperation to believe Jamie is really okay. Curiosity about how the hell this happened in the first place. Questions there's no way he'll be able to ask calmly—not yet, at least—so it seems he's opting not to ask them at all.

It seems an eternity before Warren finally huffs a defeated, "Damn it, Jamie."

Jamie makes himself draw a long, steadying breath before he says, "Victor's a good man, Dad."

Warren pushes up out of his seat with an inarticulate growl, rising to his feet so forcefully that the momentum shoves his vacated chair back with a scrape. He strides to restless motion, pacing wordlessly for several jerky seconds. With every step, he glares at the floor so hard that it's a marvel the varnished wood doesn't catch fire.

All the Way Home I'll Be Warm

Finally, Warren stops in front of the window. He shoves both hands into his pockets and stares out across the snowy backyard, as though in this fraught and shaken moment he can't bear to look at his son.

It's not technically a dismissal. Jamie's not sure what it is. A stalemate, maybe. This business between them is far from complete, but Jamie can't shake the sense that even if he stays right here—even if he argues with his father until sunset—he won't make any headway past the stiff set of narrow shoulders and the tight clench of Warren's jaw.

So Jamie stands from his own chair, far more quietly. When Warren's only reaction is to visibly tense, Jamie moves for the door.

"He can't stay here." Warren's voice calls out and catches him at the threshold to the hall. "I won't have him in my house. That's not negotiable."

"Kicking him out won't keep me away from him."

This time Warren doesn't answer, and Jamie silently completes his retreat.

*

He finds Victor a few minutes later, sitting on the topmost step of the wide front porch, bundled against the cold and watching the street with a distant look in his eyes. Jamie burrows deep into his own layers of winter gear, and steps out onto the porch despite a wind so biting it quickly makes his cheeks burn. The sun has slipped behind a cluster of sullen gray clouds.

Jamie settles himself on the step beside Victor—snuggles close when Victor raises an arm in invitation—then breathes a low sigh when that arm wraps around his shoulders.

"You okay?" Victor asks.

"Yeah. Furious, but okay." Jamie nuzzles in and inhales Victor's reassuring scent. "What about you?"

Victor huffs a wry, flattened sort of chuckle. "I'm a little worse for wear, but I'll live."

"He had no right to talk to you that way."

"He was angry." Victor's shrug jostles Jamie. "This hasn't been my best morning, but I imagine Warren didn't enjoy it much either."

Jamie doesn't want to listen to Victor defending Warren Phipps. He doesn't want to catch even the faintest hint that Victor might think the insults were justified. Bad enough he had to listen to them in the first place. But something tells Jamie if he tries to keep arguing the point, Victor will just dig in harder.

So he lets the subject drop and instead asks, in as light a tone as he can manage, "Did you really call me a hot young twink?"

"No," Victor says, but he sounds sheepish. "I called you a gorgeous young man with a clever mouth."

"That's just fancier words for the same thing."

"Then yes. Apparently I did call you a hot young twink. No wonder your dad wants to throttle me."

Jamie's attempt at levity evaporates at this reminder of Warren's rage, despite the teasing tone of Victor's observation. He hates knowing his own actions have driven a wedge between two men who have been friends longer than he's been alive. Even furious as he is at his dad, he hates that he's caused him pain. And Victor must be feeling all sorts of answering hurt, regardless of the fact that he walked into this with his eyes fully open to the consequences.

"I'm sorry," Jamie says softly, tipping his head against Victor's shoulder. "I tried to convince him, but he won't let you stay."

"It doesn't matter. He's right about that, at least. I can't stay here."

"Where will you go?"

"I have other friends in the area. And enough money to find an apartment on short notice. This close to so many universities, plenty of places offer a month-to-month lease."

Jamie eases back far enough to blink at him. "Wait. Were you already planning for this?" These past couple days, with Warren out of town and so much uncertainty about how to broach the subject, has Victor been doing research and bracing for the worst?

"I figured I wouldn't be welcome once Warren found out, no matter how we broke the news. It seemed prudent to have a backup plan." Victor bumps their foreheads together, an easy gesture that somehow manages to dispel the worst of Jamie's anxieties.

"That's why you're out here," Jamie realizes. "You're leaving."

"I won't go far." Victor speaks the words like a promise. "And I didn't want to go without making sure you're okay. I'll be visiting some friends across the river first, but then I've scheduled a few showings for this afternoon. I'll text you an address when I have one."

"What, you're not coming back for dinner?" Jamie tries to make the question a shared joke, but it comes out too raw. Hell, *Jamie* doesn't particularly want to be here for dinner tonight. Of course Victor needs to be anywhere else.

"Hell no," Victor says, and if his light tone is a little forced, at least there's a faint shimmer of real humor in it. "You're on your own for this one. I plan on keeping my distance for a while."

"From them." Jamie can't quite resist the need to clarify and insist. "Not from me."

"Not from you," Victor allows with reassuring ease.

"If you find a place today," Jamie says more hesitantly, "can I come stay with you? Or at least visit? Tonight?"

"I'd like that." Then Victor reels him in for a kiss. Slow, careful, lingering. It tastes like a promise, and Jamie leans in with answering intensity. He needs Victor to know he's still sure of this. Of them.

He's not going anywhere.

"I should hit the road," Victor murmurs when they break apart. He kisses Jamie's forehead again. "Stay out of trouble."

"Sure," Jamie agrees. He's never been very good at finding trouble anyway, present circumstances aside. Maybe he'll call some local friends himself. Bother Sarita. Hide out at his favorite coffee shop. Conjure some excuse to be out of the house for a few hours.

It's going to be a long, *long* day.

chapter fourteen

In the end, Jamie lasts less than an hour at home before restlessness drives him out into the wider world. It's a coward's retreat, running away while Anika is still off at brunch—assuming she hasn't cut her socializing short. There's no way Warren has refrained from texting or calling her in the wake of the morning's confrontation, to share all the enraged and sordid details. Jamie doesn't relish the thought of them teaming up against him.

So he packs up his computer and a book he won't be able to focus on, then takes himself to the nearest coffee shop.

He doesn't have anything to work on for school, but he still manages to while away most of the morning without going stir crazy, lingering over donuts and chai lattes until the place gets busy enough to make him feel guilty for monopolizing a table. From there, despite the cold and the weight of the satchel across his shoulder, Jamie takes a long and aimless walk. Sarita doesn't answer when he tries to call—but she calls him back just as he's starting to get hungry enough to consider slipping into a nearby diner for hash browns and pancakes.

She listens to his shaky update, then murmurs a gruff, "God damn, babe, that sucks. You doing okay?"

"Sure," he says, even though her easy acceptance and support are doing complicated things to his heart.

"Are you *actually* doing okay?"

"Maybe," he admits more honestly. "I've locked horns with Dad before, but today was... I've never seen him like this. It's not the first time he's acted like I'm still an unreliable teenager with bad judgment, but it's never been over something this important. I don't know how to convince him."

He's not looking forward to facing his mom either, but that anxiety pales next to the crisis with Warren.

"Do you need to convince him?" Sarita asks, surprisingly softly. "He can't stop you from dating Victor."

Jamie considers this. He weighs her question long and hard before answering. "I want him to be okay with it. Eventually. I need him to at least try. He's allowed to be surprised and angry, but what if he hates Victor forever? I don't want that to happen because of me."

"Not to be harsh," Sarita says quietly, "but I don't think that's something you have any say in."

Sarita's never been the sort of friend to offer empty reassurances, so Jamie ends the call still just as anxious as he was before. He feels better in other ways though. More settled in his own skin, if not precisely calm. And when he steps into the diner and claims a seat at the counter, the tightness in his belly is significantly more from hunger than nerves.

He stays out until nearly seven o'clock, through an afternoon of insufficient distraction and then dinner in the company of his local friends. But Jamie needs to go home eventually. And when he does, he's not surprised to find his mom waiting to ambush him. It's not like the text updates he sent her about his plans did anything to change the fact that they need to talk. He told his dad as much truth as he could tolerate, and perhaps a little more. But Anika Phipps deserves better than a secondhand report. She deserves an actual conversation, explanations, reassurances. She'll be worried.

And Jamie's efforts at avoiding her all day won't have alleviated her concerns.

She's already standing in the mudroom when he slips into the house, her petite frame suited up in a thick winter coat, her ears and throat covered with a soft headband and scarf in matching red.

"Let's go for a walk," she says, nudging him right back in the direction of the door before he has a chance to shed his jacket. "It's lovely outside."

"It's freezing outside," Jamie protests. He should know, he spent the whole day dithering out there off-and-on, and now that the sun has set it's even worse. It's snowing and atmospheric, sure—Jamie can concede that the outdoors is very pretty tonight—and the wind has died down. But it's still uncomfortably cold, and

All the Way Home I'll Be Warm

Jamie doesn't relish the thought of being outside.

Then again, he had his chance to come home during daylight and do this when it would have been more pleasant. He sets down his messenger bag and allows himself to be guided out the front door.

"All right, yes, it's freezing," Anika agrees. "But it's snowing, and the neighbors still have their lights up."

"Where are we walking?" Jamie asks when he reaches the sidewalk in front of the house.

"That way." Anika gestures toward the west, in a half-hearted wave that makes it clear the destination doesn't really matter. There's a cluster of local businesses a few blocks that direction, and a lake eight blocks beyond that, but the other direction is just as scenic, especially on a winter night full of houses covered in radiant decorations.

It takes Jamie several trudging steps before he can make himself say, "I'm guessing you have questions."

"Some," Anika says, in a tone that means *very, very many*. But for a while longer, she simply walks beside him in silence. Jamie can't decide if she's gathering her thoughts or waiting for him to break. Could be either. His mom is not above strategic manipulation, and while she rarely uses the skill against him, he has certainly experienced it over the years.

Jamie knew he wouldn't get away with not talking to her about this. He knew their conversation would have to come sooner rather than later. Just last night he was prepared to tell both of his parents simultaneously, all confidence and bravado. But this isn't how anything was supposed to go, and suddenly he's not ready at all, especially in the wake of his dad's incredulous wrath. He was prepared to do this on his own terms, with Victor. Instead, he's approaching Anika at a disadvantage, and he doesn't like it one bit.

He forces himself to wait, if not patiently, then at least quietly as his mom mulls through complicated thoughts. They move at a sedate pace along a sidewalk bathed one moment in the white glow of a streetlamp, the next in a rainbow patchwork from a tree at the edge of the pavement, the next in a golden scatter from a string of icicle lights.

All the Way Home I'll Be Warm

It actually is a beautiful night for a walk. Even the cold isn't as bad as Jamie feared, now that they're moving. He's bundled up warmly enough, with his puffy coat and earmuffs, his scarf wrapped multiple times around his neck and face. The Christmas lights are lovely and ethereal—there's not a single inflatable Santa to be seen on the entire block—and Jamie walks wordlessly beside his mom for a very long time, their footsteps careful along the icy sidewalk.

He could almost pretend this is just a normal outing, if not for the thrum of anticipation twisting beneath his skin.

Jamie refuses to break the quiet. He's not going to deflect the inevitable interrogation by chattering about other things. He will allow himself the dignity of waiting for his mom to say what she means to say, even if keeping silent is more difficult than it has any right to be.

When Anika finally speaks, she doesn't beat around the bush. "I'm sure you can imagine the state your father's in."

Jamie's gut twists at the reminder. "He had no right to talk about Victor that way."

"He was shocked and angry." Anika sounds wry and calm, which just makes it downright disorienting when she adds in the same unflappable tone, "and quite frankly, so am I." Jamie looks at her more closely, and his stomach clenches tighter at the glint in her eyes—the calm wrath written across her face and mirroring her words.

"Mom," he pleads. He feels suddenly helpless, less sure than ever how to convince her that he and Victor deserve a chance to prove they aren't making a mistake.

Not that she gets any more say in Jamie's love life than Warren does. But he'd like to harbor at least a little hope of his parents eventually accepting his relationship. He doesn't want to spend his life holding the pieces of his heart in separate quadrants that can't afford to overlap. Even more desperately, he doesn't want to be the wedge that drives Victor and Warren permanently apart.

There's nothing he can do on that front, though. Whether their friendship is strong enough to withstand this, it's up to Victor and Warren to navigate the uncomfortable circumstances and accusations of betrayal.

God, this shit is complicated.

All the Way Home I'll Be Warm

"Why didn't you tell me?" Anika slows her stride as though to study an especially intricate diamond pattern of white string lights arrayed across a large house.

"There was nothing to tell." Jamie feels like a liar even though it's mostly true. "I'm sure Dad doesn't believe me, but we haven't been sneaking around this whole time. We only figured everything out two days ago." This too is splitting hairs. Jamie's been in over his head, almost from the start. He kissed Victor two days ago, but they've been dancing around this thing for the entire duration of Victor's visit, and there's also the matter of Mayworth setting them on the path in the first place.

But the assertion is also honest, despite all that. And fucking hell, even if they'd been sneaking around—even if Jamie had spent every night in Victor's bed—it's not like that would mean weeks or months of deception. It's been ten days. *Ten days* since they met, and fewer that they've been together under Warren and Anika's roof.

God, how has it only been ten days?

"You've been spending a lot of time with him," Anika says in a painfully cautious tone, resuming a quicker pace down the sidewalk.

Jamie matches her stride. "Of course I have. It's Christmas break. We're living in the same house."

"You and I are living in the same house, and I've barely seen you," Anika points out, cool and a little biting.

Jamie flinches, but he makes himself answer truthfully. "I said we weren't sneaking around. Doesn't mean I haven't been distracted."

"And Victor? Has he also been distracted?" Anika doesn't give him a chance to answer this obvious rhetorical question. There's a brush of angry steel beneath her quiet tone when she asks, "How did he approach you?"

Jamie burns at the implication, subtler than Warren's accusations, that Victor manipulated him. Anika is drawing the same ugly conclusion—that Victor somehow took advantage of him—that Jamie has been a victim in this situation, rather than the enthusiastic instigator at every turn. He hates the aspersions thrown on Victor's character, when the man has only ever been sweet and soft and careful.

All the Way Home I'll Be Warm

"He didn't approach me." Jamie's hackles are rising, and he finds himself unable to keep an answering anger out of his voice. "*I* pursued *him*." Everything that's happened between them has been agonizingly mutual, but Jamie still made the first move in that bar, before he knew who Victor was. Jamie kept right on hoping, even after Victor laid down an express boundary. Jamie invited Victor into his bed, and he has not regretted his decision for a single moment since. Even in the face of inevitable confrontations, Victor Leone is the one thing he's sure about.

They've been moving quickly—more quickly than Jamie has moved with any other romantic relationship in his life—but he hasn't lost track of how they got here.

He glances at his mom and finds her chewing on her lower lip, her gaze gone distant. Anika's momentum halts entirely a moment later, and Jamie drifts to a stop beside her. Wary. Braced for impact.

When her pensive silence stretches too long, he blurts, "*What?*"

Anika folds her arms over her chest and admits, "I'm trying to decide if my next question is too intrusive."

Jamie's shoulders bunch toward his ears. "You can always ask and find out. If it's offensive, I'll just go home."

"Jamie," Anika chides.

"Don't say my name like I'm being unreasonable. If you're nervous about asking the question, it's probably going to piss me off. I won't promise not to be offended." He swallows hard. "Ask whatever you want, but don't expect me to answer if you're out of line."

She studies him in the strange, soft glow of the closest Christmas lights. Her eyes are bright with reflected illumination, her cheeks rosy from the cold. Her mouth presses into an unhappy line that tips downward at one corner, but Jamie keeps his own gaze level. He refuses to be intimidated.

Or at least, he refuses to give any outward sign.

With uncharacteristic hesitation, Anika asks, "I'd like to know how this happened. How you went so quickly from not knowing Victor at all, to being romantically involved with him."

All the Way Home I'll Be Warm

Jamie stares at her, almost too perplexed to feel defensive. "Dad didn't tell you about Mayworth?"

"Of course he told me about Mayworth." Anika waves a hand dismissively, an inkling of frustration leaking through the measured caution of her expression. "But after that. After you both knew. I would very much like to understand how Victor could have looked at you, of all people, with that kind of intent. For heaven's sake, Jamie, he's been friends with your father longer than you've been alive"

"I'm *not a child*," Jamie snaps, angry and exasperated.

"That's not what I'm saying." Anika holds her ground with maddening calm. "I'm saying that, on top of the fact that he is vastly older than you, the additional... complications... of the situation should have been a deterrent."

"Haven't you ever been attracted to someone in spite of shitty circumstances?"

"Yes," she concedes. "But never in a situation quite so bewildering as this. Not all attractions need to be acted on."

"This one did." The retort, sharp and impulsive, crackles with frustration. He hates the implication that he's the irrational one here. That his feelings for Victor are somehow invalid because of the inconvenient facts surrounding them.

"Why?" Anika asks.

"Why did you fall in love with Dad?"

And god, he can actually see the unspoken retort reflected in her eyes. *That's different.* It is. It's completely different. But Anika's thoughts are whirling obvious and bright behind her expression, and Jamie realizes how much he has just admitted. He can see his mom realizing too, recognizing how much of Jamie's heart is already wrapped up in Victor—and how truly nonexistent her chances of talking him down.

It doesn't matter if she thinks he's being foolish and impulsive. She doesn't get to condemn his feelings.

Warren probably would not have managed to hold his tongue in her place, but Anika clearly understands how close she is to a disastrous misstep.

Finally, with such a deliberate air of diplomacy that it's almost insulting, she asks, "Are you in love with Victor?"

Yes, Jamie's soul howls, instinctive and sure.

All the Way Home I'll Be Warm

Instead of answering the question, Jamie makes himself shrug and counters, "Haven't I got just as much right as anybody to figure that out for myself?" Because he needs to be smart if he's going to convince his parents to trust his judgment. He needs them to back off and acknowledge that he knows his own heart better than they possibly can. He needs them to respect his decisions.

Anika watches him with piercing intensity. "And are you so confident Victor feels the same?"

Jamie's eyes narrow. "Getting intrusive now."

"I'm allowed to worry. I don't want to see you hurt."

"It's not your job to protect me from getting my heart broken." Jamie wants to storm off, back towards home. He wants to shout until she actually listens. He wants to text Victor and ask to be whisked away somewhere, anywhere that isn't here. Instead, he swallows down his frustration and says, as calmly as he can manage, "I don't need your permission to pursue a relationship. I'm sure of Victor. But even if I'm dead-ass wrong about him… I'm allowed to make my own mistakes."

Anika falls quiet. Still watchful, but closed off in a way she wasn't a moment ago. Jamie can't tell what's going through her head now, and he's still in the dark when she faces forward and continues along the sidewalk. Her wordless pace leaves Jamie to decide whether he's going to follow her or storm home.

He waffles for only a second before falling into step, but it's a close call. He's still thrumming with resentment as he grudgingly matches her pace.

"I apologize," she says at last. Nothing more. No attempt to justify herself. Just a stubborn calm beneath silent snowfall, allowing the apology to stand on its own.

Jamie could keep arguing. He still feels riled and ready for a fight. But he won't gain any ground that way. He certainly won't get any closer to convincing his mom to take him seriously.

So he stuffs his hands into the pockets of his coat and says, "Thanks." Then lets the quiet hold.

*

All the Way Home I'll Be Warm

True to his word, Victor texts him an address that night. It comes through not long after Jamie and Anika return from their icy, awkward standoff of a walk, and Jamie immediately texts back to ask if he can come over.

Of course Victor says yes.

Jamie ducks his head into the abandoned guest room before he goes, just in case there's anything that still needs collecting, but Victor must've been back at some point to pack his things and make a more permanent retreat. His luggage is gone, the bed perfectly made, the little desk by the window empty of charging cables. There's not so much as a sock forgotten in a corner, and Jamie finds it disconcerting how much it feels like Victor was never here.

He doesn't waste time pondering the empty guest room, and almost forgets to mention to his mom that he's going out, in his rush out the door. Jamie barely notices the icy air and bright moon as he climbs into his car. It takes every scrap of concentration he can muster just to keep his focus on the road while he drives, and by the time he parks on the street in front of his destination—an old quad-style apartment building, all red brick and weathered windows—he's so restless he could crawl right out of his skin.

His fingers fly over the screen of his phone, sending a text to announce his arrival before stepping out of the warm car and into the chilly night. When he reaches the front door of the building, he doesn't even need to ring the bell. Victor's already standing there in the open doorway, backlit by a bright bulb in the entry hall that leaves his face in darkness. Despite the shadows, Jamie's sure the man is smiling. Victor wears charcoal gray pants and a squashy sweater, and somehow the effect makes him look both sexy and adorable at once.

Which is not the slightest bit fair, but Jamie's not complaining. The sight of him goes a long way toward settling the shaky feeling that followed Jamie through his entire drive. And when Victor scoops him into a hug, melting into the embrace is the easiest thing Jamie's ever done.

"Missed you," he mumbles into the soft fabric of Victor's shirt.

All the Way Home I'll Be Warm

Victor hums an acknowledging sound and doesn't tease him about the fact that it's only been a day.

The apartment is on the second floor, small and a little bit ramshackle, cozy against the winter wind. The space is furnished sparsely, but it's comfortable enough, and Jamie wonders idly if Victor bought furniture today or if the place came equipped with everything.

"Go on." Victor puts a hand to the small of Jamie's back and nudges him toward the couch, which is wide and gray and really does look inviting. "I'll make some tea to warm you up."

"I don't need tea." Jamie captures Victor's hand, intercepting him before he can disappear toward the kitchen. "Just… Sit with me? Please?"

There's a television of modest size sitting on a sturdy cabinet across from the couch, but Victor doesn't offer to turn it on as they settle in, side by side. Jamie curls close, unselfconscious, and he breathes a quiet sigh when Victor's arm wraps around his shoulders. The tension bleeds out of him by grateful degrees, and he tucks an arm around Victor's waist. Calmer now. Breathing slowly.

"Better?" Victor asks, and though he's obviously aiming for a teasing tone, the word comes out too sincere.

"Much better," Jamie agrees gamely.

"I was surprised you weren't there when I stopped by to collect my things."

Jamie frowns, although tucked as he is into the crook of Victor's shoulder there's no way his expression is visible. "Sorry. I was avoiding my parents. Taking the coward's way out."

Victor's chest shakes with a fleeting huff of laughter. "I suppose I can't blame you for that." And then, more serious, "I talked to Anika while I was there, just long enough to give back my key. It was probably the most surreal conversation I've had in my life."

"Was she more civil than Dad, at least?" Jamie eases himself reluctantly back, unwilling to pull entirely out of Victor's arms but needing to see his face, to make sure he's all right.

"Yes." A spark of contradictory humor glints in Victor's eyes. "It was impressive, honestly. I've never had such a polite conversation with someone who so clearly wanted to strangle me."

All the Way Home I'll Be Warm

Jamie grimaces, and it feels like wishful thinking when he says, "She'll come around. I talked to her tonight."

"She's got every right to worry about you. I hope it was a good conversation." The words tilt up in pitch right at the end, more question than statement, and Jamie considers.

"I honestly don't know if it did any good. I tried. I really tried to make her understand, and I think she heard me, but I don't know if it's enough. And Dad's avoiding me almost as hard as I'm avoiding him, so... God. I didn't mean to make such a mess of this." And then, as though his mouth is moving independently of his brain, Jamie hears himself ask, "Why do you want to be with me?"

Victor blinks at him with obvious surprise, spine straightening and expression baffled as he puts a sliver of space between them on the couch. "How could anyone not want to be with you? You're sweet. You're kind. You're too clever for your own good. I was a goner the second you started talking to me in that bar."

Jamie's face burns hot, and his pulse speeds. He doesn't let himself flinch away, no matter how powerful the tidal wave of emotion rolling through him. "But now you know I'm a bad idea."

"No. Complicated, maybe. But *never* a bad idea. Don't you dare think that. You, Jamie Phipps, are the best idea I've ever had."

"Yeah?" Jamie feels ridiculous for not even realizing how desperately he needed this reassurance.

For a long time, Victor simply watches him, silent and intent, so focused that Jamie all but forgets how to breathe. There is a contradictory and thoughtful ferocity in the way Victor's gaze holds him trapped. Jamie chews on his lower lip and fights not to ask what Victor is thinking about. He finds himself reluctant to interrupt whatever is going on behind Victor's eyes.

At last, Jamie's patience is rewarded when Victor asks, "Do you want to know the moment I realized keeping my distance from you was a losing battle?"

Jamie wants very much to answer with actual words, but there's too much emotion caught in his throat. All he manages is a strangle sound, which thankfully Victor takes for a yes. Victor's gaze cuts down to where Jamie's hand rests on his chest, and he covers it with his own, twining their fingers together with dizzying care.

"I saw you wrapping presents on Christmas Eve, before everyone started getting ready for all the big dinner stuff. Just. This whole mountain of gifts you volunteered to take care of, because Anika didn't have time. I wasn't spying on you or anything. Just saw you working and you were obviously hating every minute of it. I wanted to offer to help."

Jamie gives Victor's fingers a squeeze. "I wouldn't have turned down help. I hate wrapping presents. I'm awful at it."

Victor doesn't confirm this assessment, though he saw plenty of examples of Jamie's terrible wrapping ability on Christmas morning. He only gives Jamie's hand an answering squeeze and continues. "You were working on an unreasonably huge box when I spotted you. Must've been that ridiculous kitchen play set. You obviously wanted to light the whole thing on fire."

"Understatement," Jamie agrees. He plans on holding a grudge about it at least until next Christmas. "That thing was the worst."

"But you didn't finish wrapping it," Victor says. "At least, not that I saw. You had this massive piece of paper lined up and ready to go, and it looked so precarious—and before I could offer to help, May ran in looking for you. I don't remember what she was so excited about, but she was shouting and moving too fast, and next thing I knew the wrapping paper was in tatters, the box had hit the ground so hard it sounded like a meteor impact, and May was crying."

"She wasn't hurt," Jamie rushes to reassure, wondering how this can possibly tie in to what Victor offered to tell him. "The box scared her when it fell."

"I know." Victor's voice carries the audible trace of a smile. "That's my point. You didn't let her get hurt, and you didn't get angry. You just scooped her right up to make sure she was okay. You were so sweet about it, I damn near melted through the floor."

Jamie wants to argue that it wasn't a big deal. Anyone else in the house would've done the same. May's a good kid, who deserves good things, and she didn't mean any harm. But Victor knows all this. And he's still saying these things like the moment was some sort of revelation, and the thing is... Jamie gets it. He lost any hope of resisting Victor over the same small, sweet moments. Seeing Victor like that. Soft and good and kind.

Those were the moments that catapulted Jamie from attraction to crush, and from crush to something infinitely more powerful.

Why shouldn't Victor have fallen the exact same way?

"*Fuck*," Jamie breathes, and surges forward in a rush, climbing astride Victor's lap as the thought of any space at all between them becomes suddenly intolerable. He needs to feel Victor everywhere—or at the very least solid against him, just like this—and he covers Victor's smiling mouth with a kiss to convey all the things he can't imagine putting into words.

Powerful arms circle his waist and hold him close, and Victor hums an approving sound.

"Can I sleep here tonight?" Jamie asks, when at last he has the fortitude to pull away.

"Of course you can." Victor kisses the corner of his mouth, light and quick. "Any night you want."

chapter fifteen

Jamie doesn't sleep very well, despite being exactly where he wants to be. He's not nearly exhausted enough this time to override the fact that he's used to sleeping alone. But he can't bring himself to mind all the times he finds himself woken by the unfamiliar heat of a shared bed, or the slight movements of a body sleeping beside him. More than once he takes the opportunity to squirm closer, burying himself in Victor's arms and all but purring at how safe he feels.

He keeps waking up on his own side of Victor's big bed, restless sleeper that he is. But the pleased ember deep inside him continues to burn incandescent, and his fatigue in the morning can't compete with his satisfaction at starting the day with drowsy kisses.

Jamie sleeps at Victor's place the next night too. And the night after that. There's a stubbornness to the arrangement born not just of a desire for closeness, but caught up in an irrational fear that maybe January is all they'll have. What if, despite the desperate weight in Jamie's heart, circumstances bite them in the ass and all of this turns out to be temporary? What if he goes back to school and Victor slips between his fingers, completely out of reach?

Jamie does his best not to acknowledge these fears. His life is his own to shape. He won't lose Victor if he simply refuses to let go.

January creeps stubbornly by, and even with Victor's grounding presence in his life—even bouncing awkwardly back and forth between his parents' house and Victor's cozy apartment—the passage of days brings with it an undeniable rumble of cabin fever. Jamie is an overambitious student on the cusp of finishing college and starting grad school. He hasn't had a January free of obligation since he was a kid, and he's never been a fan of winter. Of course he finds himself at loose ends, with no homework to do, no applications to fill out, no essays to write.

All the Way Home I'll Be Warm

He spends more time with his local friends. By the second week, he's meeting Victor's friends too, which brings inevitable awkwardness since many of them know Warren Phipps. Even the folks who look askance at them are diplomatic about it, though. Jamie goes in braced for more dramatic reactions, and is relieved at not having to defend their relationship to people Victor counts as friends.

The night he invites Victor to a party of his own crowd, Jamie is shocked—and delighted—when the answer is an immediate yes.

For all that Jamie has spent plenty of time in public at Victor's side, there is something powerful and unexpectedly thrilling about arriving at Tamika and Andrew's place—a small house in a stretch of neighborhood between two university campuses—and introducing Victor as his boyfriend. No one so much as raises an eyebrow in the moment, though a couple of people corner Jamie alone later to ask nosy questions. *How did you meet him? Is he rich? Why didn't you tell us your boyfriend is so much older than you? Dude, where'd you find a guy that hot, you don't even date.*

"I date!" Jamie protests to that last one, and only gets an exasperated snort in return.

He manages to lose track of Victor, in the course of bouncing between groups and conversations. He would feel guilty about it, if not for the fact that when he texts to check in, he gets no reply. *Hey, you still good? Let me know if you want to leave.* If Victor is lost and bored in a quiet corner somewhere, Jamie won't make him stay at a party he's not enjoying. Jamie's having a pleasant time, but he would honestly rather be spending time with Victor than anyone else in this over-crowded house.

It's this fact that sends him on an actual search, two red plastic cups of root beer in hand.

"He was headed downstairs last I saw him," someone says, when Jamie interrupts an animated argument about violin makers to ask if anyone has seen Victor.

So Jamie heads for the stair off the main hall that leads into a finished basement. He hears excited shouting as soon as he nudges the door open with his hip, and the volume only rises as he makes his way down carpeted steps. Laughter and taunting, and even before Jamie rounds the corner into the noisy room, he can tell they're playing video games. Something on an old-school console, full of silly cars and ridiculous projectiles. Exactly the kind of game Jamie's always been terrible at.

There's one big couch at the center of the room, over-full with the four players whose cars are vying for supremacy on an enormous television screen. A dozen other people sit throughout the rest of the room—on pillows or bean bags or a couple of folding chairs—heckling and hollering encouragements.

The action on the screen is far too chaotic for Jamie to make sense of, but from the commentary flying around the room, he quickly figures out Victor is winning.

The race ends with a flourish and an ear-splitting chorus of groans and cheers.

"Rematch!" demands Andrew from one end of the couch, tossing his controller to the ground in a huff of indignation.

"You've already had three rematches," counters someone from the floor. "Give someone else a chance to get their ass handed to them."

Jamie is standing almost directly behind Victor, and yet Victor must sense his arrival, because he twists around to look over his shoulder—and there's not even the faintest suggestion of surprise in the quirk of his mouth and the crinkling corners of his eyes. "Sorry guys, I'm out," Victor says, turning around to hand his controller to the nearest bean bag occupant and standing from his spot at the center of the couch. "Thanks for the game."

A cacophony of protests follows his retreat, but he pays them no mind as he joins Jamie at the base of the stairs. The sparkle in Victor's eyes is enough to take Jamie's breath away, and he bites his lip as he hands over one of the root beers.

"Thanks." Victor leans up and in to press a kiss to Jamie's cheek. He speaks low, not secretive, but just for Jamie, when he asks, "You enjoying the party?"

"Yeah." Jamie grins. "Apparently not as much as you, though. Didn't know you were a video game champion."

Victor shrugs. "We had a couple different consoles on base. You think I spent all my downtime lifting weights and playing online chess?"

All the Way Home I'll Be Warm

"Guess not." Jamie reaches for Victor's hand, and his smile turns softer at how easily their fingers tangle together. "You want to head out soon?"

"Whenever." Victor shrugs. "I like your friends. They're good kids."

Jamie's eyes narrow, but he doesn't even need to protest before Victor offers him a chagrined look.

"Sorry. I didn't mean… They're not kids. Just younger than my usual crowd." He says this with a wry smile and sheepish air that acknowledges *Jamie* is younger than his usual crowd too. It's ground they've already covered. They don't need to retread it here.

Easy enough to relent and let Victor off the hook, especially when Jamie's just relieved the evening's been enjoyable for both of them. "Okay," he says. He takes a sip of root beer, then tugs at Victor's hand. "Come on. Let's go back upstairs." He'll drag Victor with him on one last circuit through the crowd, to say goodbye instead of vanishing into the night like phantoms, and then they can head home.

"Hey." Victor stops him on the stairs—a fleeting moment of privacy—and tugs Jamie into a real kiss, quick and sweet. Jamie presses into him, subsiding only reluctantly. He meets the fond glint in Victor's eyes with a wordless spark of heat, then lets himself be tugged right back into motion as Victor continues up the stairs.

*

The closer the end of January looms, the more Jamie wants to spend every waking hour at Victor's new apartment. He resists the urge, despite how uncomfortable he finds existing in his parents' house right now. He still sleeps in Victor's bed most nights, but he is also painfully aware that he won't convince his parents of anything by avoiding them completely.

Twice he finds himself left behind when Anika—once via phone call and once by turning up unannounced on Victor's doorstep—invites Victor on long walks, for conversations that cannot possibly be pleasant for either of them. Jamie tries not to rankle at the fact that he is expressly not invited. His presence wouldn't help. The conversations may be about him, at their core, but his voice isn't the one Anika needs to hear right now.

He hates how tense they both are when they return from these wintery jaunts, quiet and off-balance and disinclined to tell him what he's missed. But the fact that Anika keeps reaching out seems important, and Jamie chooses to be grateful she's making an effort.

Warren is a different story, quiet in a way that speaks more to sullen rage than awkward misgivings. Jamie tries a dozen times to talk to him, but the effort never gets him far. Maybe his voice is the wrong one here, too. Warren is almost certainly worried about Jamie, protective father that he is, but Jamie isn't the crux of the problem. No input from Jamie can repair the breach between Warren and Victor. As far as the betrayal between friends is concerned, Jamie is an outside party. It's not his place to ask for Warren's forgiveness.

It still hurts. More than anything, Jamie wants to help, and he hates how little he can actually do.

The day he arrives at Victor's apartment and hears his dad's voice through the front door, Jamie nearly falls over from the shock. Even more startling is the resigned calm that carries through Warren's voice, each word clipped and unhappy, but steady in a way Jamie wouldn't have anticipated.

"Are you in love with my son?"

Jamie has already put the key in the lock, and he freezes with his hand on the doorknob, keeping perfectly still.

"I've known him a month," Victor says, and the answer is as good as the *yes* pulsing like a beacon in Jamie's chest. If the answer were *no*, Victor would have spoken bluntly instead of dodging the question. "Would you even believe me, if I told you I was already in love with him?"

The sound Warren huffs is surprisingly close to a laugh, gruff and dry though it is. "Fuck no."

A thoughtful quiet extends, through which Jamie can't actually picture the expression on either man's face. Even his dad, whom he knows so well, remains a cipher within the contours of Jamie's mind. Probably frowning, but with what nuance? Stubborn anger? Grudging forgiveness? Fearful confusion? It bothers Jamie to not know—though not enough to coax him forward and through the door.

All the Way Home I'll Be Warm

Finally Victor breaks the silence, speaking low and earnest. "Believe this, then. I want to be a good partner, for as long as he'll have me."

Exasperated wrath surges in Jamie's chest, so hot that he misses the next murmured words. By the time he tunes back in, the conversation has turned another direction. Quieter, making Jamie strain to hear the words being exchanged.

"I don't know that I'll ever be able to forgive you." Warren sounds heartbroken now, overriding the low thrum of anger still present in his voice. "I can't even promise to try. You get how fucked this is, right?"

"I know I hurt you," Victor says. "And I truly am sorry for that. I went about this all wrong."

Warren's answer is a bitter rasp of laughter. "There's no *right way* to go about this, Vic. We're talking about my son. You can't possibly think there was any chance I'd approve of you sleeping with him, for fuck's sake."

Victor murmurs something too low for Jamie to hear, prompting Warren to lower his voice too. Not deliberately secretive—they can't possibly have noticed he's out here—but maddeningly quiet and making it impossible to hear what they're saying. A moment later, Jamie loses track of even the softer indecipherable murmuring, and he stifles a curse as he eases closer to the door.

He's so focused on trying to figure out if they're still talking that he doesn't register the tap of footsteps approaching, and when the door swings inward beneath his hand, Jamie can't even pretend he wasn't eavesdropping.

His dad stands there blinking at him, stunned and frozen. Jamie stares back guiltily for several seconds, before finally stepping aside. It's a painfully awkward exchange, as Warren gives him a nod and a quick clap on the shoulder, and then hurries past Jamie, across the landing and down the stairs, disappearing out the front entrance without a word.

Victor's door is still open, and Jamie steps through, barely remembering to reclaim his keys on the way past. Victor himself stands near the window, posture loose, hands in his front pockets. He wears a bemused little smile, and Jamie's surprised he doesn't seem irritated about being spied on.

Jamie knocks the door shut with his hip and hangs his keys on the hook beside the light switch. Out of deference to Victor's clean floors, he kicks off his boots before flopping down onto the unsteady old armchair in the corner. The conversation replays through his mind in bits and pieces, and he draws a shaky breath as one piece in particular snags on his thoughts like a thorn.

"*For as long as I'll have you*?" he demands, glaring at Victor across the apartment and folding his legs up to his chest. He wraps his arms around his knees, as though maybe he can ground himself if he holds on tight enough. "What kind of fickle asshole do you think I am?"

"I don't think you're fickle." Victor moves with remarkable efficiency, crossing the space between them in quick strides. He bypasses the couch completely, and instead kneels on the floor where Jamie's feet would be, if he weren't so thoroughly folded into the chair. "I think you're young."

"That's not the vote of confidence I was hoping for." Jamie swallows past a lump of feeling and makes himself push past the instinct to brush this aside. "Whatever you think I'm trying to... I wouldn't use you like that, Vic. I know I can be thoughtless, but I wouldn't—"

"Hey." Victor rises up onto his knees and takes both of Jamie's hands between his own. "You've *never* been thoughtless. And I know you wouldn't. That's not what I'm saying."

Jamie unfolds his legs, the better to let Victor hold onto his hands. Hell, he hadn't even realized he was anxious about this, but here he is staring into Victor's eyes, begging for reassurances he's not sure how to articulate.

"Then what are you saying?" he asks.

Victor considers him for what feels like a very long time. "I'm saying you don't need to make me any promises. Not now. Not yet." An upward twitch at the corner of his mouth tempers these words enough that they don't feel like a rejection. "This is still new for both of us. We've got a lot to figure out, no matter how much we might care for each other."

Jamie catches his lower lip between his teeth, worrying at it for a moment but ultimately failing to stop himself from blurting the quiet confession. "You know I love you, right?"

Victor's dark eyes go soft, his whole expression beaming with fondness, heat, humor, even a hint of possessiveness. Such a complicated whirlwind of emotions, and every single one of them resonates all the way through Jamie's chest, his belly clenching tight in answer. When Victor's hand touches the side of his face, Jamie nuzzles into his palm.

"I love you too, sweetheart," Victor says, and the ready sincerity of the words chases away the worst of Jamie's fears. "But I've also got decades on you. The last thing I ever want is to make you feel trapped."

What if I want to be trapped by you? Jamie resists the urge to ask this question, painfully aware that it won't get him any extra points in their discussion. Hell, if any of his friends called and told him they'd found the love of their life in someone they'd only known a matter of weeks, Jamie would be hard pressed to believe them. From a more practical vantage point, nothing about this makes sense. And little as Jamie wants to think about that view of reality right now, he can't actually fault Victor's caution.

"We're at very different places in our lives," Victor murmurs, as though answering the meandering path of Jamie's thoughts. "That doesn't mean we can't be together. But it complicates things. I'll never forgive myself if I hurt you, and the best way to make sure that doesn't happen is to be realistic about the challenges ahead."

"You were talking to Dad like you're assuming this won't last."

"Not assuming." Victor's other hand squeezes tighter where he still holds both of Jamie's. "I'm not letting you go without a fight. But if you ever want out, I won't hold you back. That's the truth your dad needs to know, if he's ever going to trust me again."

"You should come to Spokane with me." The words burst out of Jamie, sudden and jarring, and his eyes widen at the urgent plea in his own voice.

Victor blinks up at him, startled to silence.

Jamie sets both feet firmly on the ground and leans forward—so close he could kiss Victor if he wanted to—holding onto Victor's hands more tightly than ever. "I'm staying put for grad school, so I'll be there a few more years. You could move in with me while you figure out what you want to do."

Victor only looks more shocked at this explanation. "Jamie..."

All the Way Home I'll Be Warm

"It's a small apartment, but we already know we can share a bathroom without killing each other." Jamie tries to keep his tone teasing, but he can't entirely conceal the pleading ache. The thought of having Victor in his space fills him with eager longing, even if his tiny little one-bedroom apartment will be completely impractical to share. "You can still buy your own place if you want. Or we can look for a bigger apartment together. But no matter what, house hunting will be easier if you already have somewhere to stay, right? I mean... assuming you'd be okay with living in Washington."

"You're serious?" A note of awe has crept into Victor's voice.

"Of course I'm serious. I want you with me." Jamie swallows hard. "I'll do long distance if we need to, but couldn't we just... Once I finish grad school, we can go anywhere. Washington's as good a place as any for an existential crisis in the meantime, right?"

Victor huffs a low laugh. "I told you, it's not an existential crisis."

Jamie cracks a smile. "Soul searching, then. Washington's as good a place as any for soul searching."

"You're probably right."

Jamie's breath hitches. "So you'll come to Spokane?"

"I will," Victor agrees, and covers Jamie's relieved laugh with a kiss.

epilogue

"We're not taking your car," Victor says, in the unyielding voice of a man who refuses to be argued with. It's such an unusual tone for him to take that Jamie is honestly startled, though he makes a point of spreading the rest of the peanut butter across his toast before answering.

"It gets better mileage than yours." He nudges Victor under the table with his bare toes. "We'll be paying twice as much for gas if we take your car."

"But at least we'll get where we're going. Remind me. What happened last time you drove to the Cities in that little death trap of yours?"

"Rude," Jamie says. "You should be nicer to my little death trap. We wouldn't have met the way we did, if I'd been driving a more reliable car." He takes a bite of toast and lets his point linger. Victor's kitchen is cozy this morning, the warmest room in the house by far thanks to the oven already baking a second batch of sugar cookies. Jamie's still not sure why Victor is so insistent on baking cookies to take to Minnesota, never mind why he's baking them at seven o'clock on a Saturday morning.

Either things will go okay with Warren and Anika, or they won't; cookies won't make any difference either way.

"We're not taking your car," Victor repeats, pushing up from the table and crossing the kitchen to check on the cookies through the oven door. "It's been making a weird squeak and you still haven't taken it into the shop. There's not enough time to get it looked at before Monday."

Jamie huffs, but he knows Victor is right. "Fine. We'll take your beast of a car instead. But you have to make it up to me." He glances over and finds Victor watching him from several feet away, arms crossed over a festive red sweatshirt, face twisted into an expression of grudging amusement. Victor's eyes flash with fondness, and he leans one hip against the counter.

"Make it up to you how?"

All the Way Home I'll Be Warm

Jamie sets down his toast in favor of a long swallow of orange juice. "Surprise me."

"Hmm. I suppose I might have an idea." There's something serious beneath the more playful edge of Victor's considering tone, and Jamie's eyes narrow. Flirtation is never far from either of their voices when they banter, but this is something more complicated. Something taut and bright and... hopeful?

Chair legs scrape on tile as Jamie pushes up from his seat. No fucking way is he keeping his distance from Victor *now*, with such a delicious mystery in sight. But Victor doesn't continue, even once Jamie gets closer. Even when Jamie draws near enough to touch—Victor unfolds his arms and tugs him into a loose hug, but still doesn't say a word.

"I'm listening." Jamie drapes his arms across Victor's shoulders and bumps their foreheads together. "Don't be a tease."

"I could call some movers and arrange for them to bring all your stuff here."

Jamie's eyes widen. "You... Really?"

It's been a year since he and Victor met. Eleven months since he dragged the man halfway across the continent. Ten months since he had to grudgingly admit it made sense for Victor to buy a place of his own, while they took the time to find their footing and build a relationship solid enough to last. Jamie didn't want Victor to move out, but even he had to admit his tiny apartment near campus wasn't a realistic space for both of them to share. When Victor announced his plan to buy a house a little farther from campus—though near enough to be a tolerable commute—and closer to the art gallery where Victor's been working almost since moving to Washington, Jamie very deliberately did not invite himself along.

He knows Victor worries about taking him for granted. He knows too that it's been healthy for them to have their own space while Jamie gets a feel for grad school.

But Jamie is also grateful that, separate spaces or not, he rarely goes more than a day or two without Victor's company. Most nights he ends up here—or Victor ends up squashed into the narrow bed in Jamie's apartment—and they maintain a balance that works for both of them, even if it does occasionally feel like they're living together already.

All the Way Home I'll Be Warm

He's more than ready to give up the unnecessary distance.

Victor's expression remains cautious, despite the hopeful glint in his eyes. "Your lease is up in March, isn't it? That's enough time to give notice. If you want to."

And oh, Jamie's heart is suddenly so full he doesn't know how to contain all this feeling. His smile spreads wide across his face, his chest going tight and warm. He crushes forward to take Victor's mouth in a greedy kiss, thrilling when Victor leans up to meet him and slides rough fingers into Jamie's sleep-tousled hair. His whole body thrums with new energy, with excitement, with a satisfaction long-delayed.

If Victor is inviting Jamie to move in, that means he's *finally sure.* No more second-guessing this thing. No more doubting Jamie's in it for good. It's not just the house. It's everything sturdy and solid between them, and the future they're going to build on that foundation.

"I'd love to move in with you," he says, breathless with the end of the kiss—needing to say it out loud. "I'll send the apartment manager my notice today. If I ask nicely, maybe he'll let me out of my lease early. Easier to find renters near a university in January than March."

Victor's answering smile is all liquid heat and soft promise. "Good. I can call to arrange the movers while we're in Minnesota." Familiar gravel rumbles in his voice, as his arms wind loosely around Jamie's waist. "And then after Christmas, I'll bring you home."

the end

about the author

Yolande Kleinn may be a shameless dreamer and a stubborn optimist, but she is also a proud purveyor of romance and erotica. Excitable, fastidious and a little eclectic, she spends every spare moment writing the stories she wants to read. If she can drag other people into the pool along with her, then so much the better.

You can find Yolande via her website:
yolandekleinn.com

other titles by yolande

AN INTIMATE CHARADE

Cargo ship captain Galin Odona is in desperate need of a contract. When a lucrative opportunity comes his way, he invites Addison Valdez—smart, stubborn, and the only Human member of his crew—to join the negotiation.

Anatoria Baell's contract is not precisely legal, and she has unconventional methods for choosing where to put her trust. Galin agrees to pose as a distant relation during a gathering at her private estate. The negotiation takes a complicated turn when Addison proclaims that Galin is not only his captain, but his mate. The hot-headed lie puts them in a tough spot, maintaining their charade for the duration.

But Galin is a terrible liar. Even worse, he's been in love with Addison for years. Now, through tight quarters and an illusion of intimacy, he must win the contract without giving himself away. The task seems monumental, but Galin cannot afford to fail.

SIMPLE AFTER ALL

Noah Fiore, contracts attorney and dedicated curmudgeon, spends every Christmas with his family on the shore of Lake Superior. It's practically tradition for his sister to invite some lonely acquaintance along for the festivities.

But this year's guest is no pity case. Riley Coto is a friend, whose warmth and charm instantly win over the collective hearts of the Fiore family— all except Noah, who remains as dour and unapproachable as ever.

Riley finds himself inexplicably drawn to Noah. Something tells him there's more to the man than stubborn work ethic and bad attitude. With Christmas fast approaching, Riley is falling for Noah, and there's nothing simple about that.

HEARTS RIGHT HERE

From road trips to isolated cabins, business partners to longtime besties, old crushes to new revelations, former bosses to dad's best friend... Delve into nine contemporary romances where friendship changes course.

Collection includes: Something Softer—Wishful Thinking—Very Close and All at Once—Just About Perfect—Running Hot—Anticipation—Matters of Heart—Right Here with Me—Put It in Writing

ASHES ON A DISTANT WIND

Before the Vrete came to Earth, Donovan Riggs was a man of faith. Now they're gone, and he's left that part of himself behind for good. In the ruinous aftermath of a war nobody won, he is simply trying to survive. With Beau Greer—a young medic who stumbled into his life and then refused to leave—Riggs travels dangerous roads between long-dead cities. Scavenging doesn't offer much of a future. It barely provides for the present. But Riggs will do anything to protect what's his.

EVERY SECOND YOU'RE ALIVE

Major Franklin Cade has spent years fighting the undead scourge that drove humanity from Earth. Now victory is in sight, but it's come at immeasurable cost. He has sacrificed everything in the line of duty—even his own heart.

For six months Lieutenant Daniel Mendoza has been missing in action. Only stubbornness and a refusal to tarnish Mendoza's memory have kept Franklin alive since losing the man he wouldn't admit he loved.

When a perilous rescue needs volunteers, he returns to the canyon where Mendoza fell. He is not prepared for the hope that ignites as he follows a fading distress signal across infested terrain. In the shadow of a deadly countdown every second is precious, but Franklin refuses to lose Mendoza again.

OPEN SKIES

After seven years working as partners, Kai and Ilsa are the best professional finders in the business. There's nothing they can't track down, no matter how unfamiliar the star system or hazardous the path. When a new client insists on accompanying the search for his daughter, Ilsa and Kai reluctantly agree. How can they refuse when Eleazar Dantes is desperate enough to pay double their usual fee?

But a high-stakes investigation is no time for distractions. Even more troublesome, when Kai realizes his true feelings for Ilsa, his timing couldn't be worse. Never mind that she doesn't seem to reciprocate: heartbreak is the least of their problems as the trail they're following grows dangerous.

With every step forward, Kai and Ilsa are more certain they won't find Eleazar's missing daughter alive.